The Ghost Towns
of Amador

by

John R. Andrews

Fresno, California — 1978

Preface

Out of the billions of dollars of the yellow metal
that the Mother Lode of California poured into the
Nation's coffers at times of great need, Amador
contributed around or just over thirty per cent. Of
all the lode counties Amador is the smallest. By
comparison with some of its neighbors it may be
labeled tiny. But if we take the position that because the area is small, what happened there is of
no importance the same iron logic would rule out
of history rocky Palestine, marble boned Attica,
and Florence, the Lily of the Arno. Of course we
do no such thing.

It has been well said:

"Better fifty years of Athens than a cycle of
Cathay."

J.R.A.

1967

ISBN 0-913548-54-5

Valley Publishers
Division of Book Publishers, Inc.
8 E. Olive Ave., Fresno, CA 93728

iv

Contents

Prologue

Any compilation of the vanished communities that sprang up in the wake of the gold strikes must be drawn from diverse sources. Among these sources are maps of the 1850's in the State and County libraries; old newspapers, some of them printed in the now vanished cities. "The Quincy Prospect," "The Lancha Plana Advertiser," and old City Directories: Yes, there are such of record of Lancha Plana and of Quincy. Property transfers and transactions that may be found in the Recorder's office.

The most productive method however is the exploration of the sites themselves. There is always discoverable the old building footings, the chimneys; mostly, but not always, fallen—the cemeteries, wells, stone boundary fences. There are quadrangular mounds of earth that were once adobe structures, now unroofed and returned to the soil from which they came by the rains of more than a century. On the other hand, there are *hornos*, outdoor ovens much used by Latin peoples, some of which may still be found intact and may be fired and operated to this day.

Near quartz outcroppings we find *arrastres*. These are primitive ore mills powered by mules. Great boulders are dragged in a circle upon a pavement of cobbles whereon the quartz was pulverized and the gold recovered. More rarely a Chile mill, the crushing being effected by two giant wheels of stone, axled by a hard wood beam and turned upon a pivot, also by mule power. In the remote canyons the ironwork of old wagons and coaches under the covering brush has somehow escaped the attention of the junkies.

1

A mine detector will turn up quantities of number nine stoves. These bear the name of a New York foundry. They were most ingeniously designed to fold and be transported by pack saddle. For some reason they have not been mentioned by the historians.

Also evident in quantity are the wrought iron hoops of the oaken containers of the Amontillado Sherry exported from the Spanish port of Jerez for centuries past. These little kegs, called *pipes* by the coopers by reason of their elongated shape, were obviously used in all conceivable ways as containers. In volume they held about three gallons and were readily transportable by pack animals.

In addition there are fragments of iron spherical kettles of various sizes; square cut nails; table forks, three tined, slender in the pattern of the 1850's oftimes with the bone handle still undecayed.

A cooking oil under the name of "Jewel" must have had wide distribution. The containers, heavily tinned, are found everywhere. Most of the labels are still readable.

Slender bottles of dark green glass, French in origin, and apparently containing wine or champagne are widely in evidence, together with stone or crockery bottles, cream colored, sometimes with tan necks, and sometimes bearing upon the bottom the word "Ale" and the point of origin Glasgow Scotland.

Crockery or stonewear appears, some obviously Chinese in origin, other types American in pattern. Judging from the fragments recovered, our ancestors must have loved fine china. Dainty and delicate bits of Dresden, Wedgewood, and De Haviland are at all sites.

In the realm of the completely vanished mention must be made of rawhide. To the American Mountain Man, Spanish Californian, Mexican, Chileno, and Spaniard, rawhide was as bamboo to the Chinese or cocoanut palm to the Polynesian. If a thing could not be made of rawhide it probably could not be made.

2

As a small boy in Old Lancha Plana and in Campo Seco I have seen water buckets, doors (made by lashing hide over pole frames), shutters, dust pans, beds, (lash a green hide over a frame, lie on it until it sets and you have your own personal form-fitting beauty-rest), chair bottoms, chair backs, table covers, cupboards, wagon bed covers. There is just no end to its uses.

In economic base, national origin, terrain, and in just about every other characteristic there was enormous variation from any standard pattern. For example: Townerville, Copper Hill, and Ranlett worked rich copper deposits. Quincy, Doschville, and Live Oak were in part agricultural. Those immediately adjacent to the Mother Lode were in part engaged in hard rock operations at an early date. Carbondale exploited lignite coal. Summit City worked silver. Doschville mined pottery clay of high ceramic value. The majority, however, were based upon placer deposits.

In elevation they ranged from Lancha Plana under 300 feet to Summit City over 8,000 feet.

In terrain they ranged from the billiard table flatness of Carbondale to cliff-hanging Rancherias and Summit City, high in the eternal snows.

To a degree, national origins may be ascertained from the names themselves. French Camp and Butte City were mainly Gallic. China Gulch needs no comment, nor does Spanish Gulch. Irishtown and Irish Hill were almost solidly the Sons of Erin. Arkansas Diggings and Arkansas Ferry; obvious. Lancha Plana, Camp O'pera, the Rancherias all Spanish-speaking folk from the Old World and the New. Misery Flat, Jackass Gulch, Clapboard Gulch, Slabtown, and Blood Gulch vividly portray the earthiness and directness of the Saxon in a moment of truth.

Methods of construction and materials used were as diverse as the lengths of time that the communities were in existence. Differing climatic conditions that had to be

3

met at differing elevations. Tents, *ramadas,* and *jacales* first sprang up in the more temperate climatic areas. Then, as winter approached, the tents were floored and even sided with boards.

The roots of the *jacales* were thatched thicker with brush. They became *cajones* by the addition of woven brush to the walls. The walls were then plastered with clay—substantially the old English wattle and daub method.

In the second stage of construction sawmills produced wide boards, framing timber, and even mill work. Workers skilled in adobe construction erected substantial buildings plastered to cream whiteness by several coats of plaster made of sand and burnt lime. At this point we must digress to pay tribute to the builders of the great lime kilns that are to be found between Volcano and the town of Sutter Creek and in the area of Lower Dry Creek. Without their product, the brick and stone structures would not have been possible.

From the magnificent stands of Sugar Pine came shakes in profusion, to roof the structures. The towns became almost permanent. In the third and final stage, brick kilns were built by the Americans. The product of these kilns together with that of the lime kilns went into beautiful edifices. Skilled masons and quarrymen from Italy, using the techniques of ancient Rome, built the great buildings with the iron doors and shutters that may still be seen in Old Volcano, Amador City, Sutter Creek, Jackson Gate, Drytown and many another Lode town.

Perhaps at this point it would be in order to mention two other techniques. One: the erection of tapia or rammed earth structures. They are amazingly resistant to demolition. An excellent example is to be found in the Chinese Joss House in Old Fiddletown; occupied and in use to this day. Two: the use of fieldstone, stratified serpentine, or indeed any available rock, coursed at random in adobe or lime mortar and then given three coats

4

of plaster; the last coat yielded a surface that in places still retains the smoothness and lustre of a china plate.

Of the frame structures, the spool work and ginger-bread of the early and High Victorian era almost no specimen survives. Just as well, perhaps. Our long hot summers and innumerable fires have taken good care of that.

With each passing year the ceaseless assault of the elements, the depredations of the vandal and hoodlum, and that arch-enemy of these ancient things the blade of the bull dozer take their toll.

The loss of these witnesses to a vanished way of life can only be described as heart-breaking.

Ground Rules

At this point some ground rules must be established as to what is a ghost town. Let us say that a ghost town is one that, once had a population of at least several hundred and now has none or no more than five. This rules out small communities like New Chicago and Buena Vista which, through all of the years, have maintained at least a shadowy identity.

No finality may ever be achieved on a subject such as this. Evidence both documentary and archaeological will continually surface. A case in point: The diary of John Doble. He was already known to our history as a Justice of the Peace in Volcano and a magistrate in Jackson. His diary was uncovered in an attic in Indiana in the early 1960's. Someone recognized its value and now we have this treasure giving light and information at exactly the period where we need it most.

Who knows when someone, in moving an old book-case in Barcelona, will come upon the diary of Great Uncle Miguel, who took the trail to California long long ago.

An old trunk in Penzance may give us letters written

by Great Grandfather from the gold camps. From anywhere on earth, at any time, additional material may and probably will appear.

As roads are widened and re-routed, new ones built, streets for subdivisions laid out; startling new evidence will be turned out.

If we wait it will be for years and generations. Of course we will never have all of it.

So let us see if we can get on with what we have at this time.

Lancha Plana

In the listing of our vanished communities, Lancha Plana on the Mokelumne River, and Quincy compete for supremacy. Which would take first place at this late date will probably never be known.

Since Lancha Plana bears the numeral one we may begin with information that has survived from its earliest days.

Mason writes that two individuals of Down East extraction appeared upon the scene in 1849 or 1850. He gives their names as Kaiser and Winter. They cut timbers and constructed a frame. Beneath it they lashed empty whiskey barrels; building a most serviceable ferry.

The fare was fifty cents. Much patronage ensued immediately and these two entreprenuers did a thriving business.

In the tongue of the miners from Sonora and Valparaiso it was referred to as "La Lancha Plana"—flat boat or ferry.

The name was applied to the mushrooming community on the north bank. And, incidentally, Spanish remained the dominant language of the area well into the twentieth century and to this day is far from extinct in the reaches south of the Mokelumne.

There is reason to believe that the earliest discoverers of these placers were guided to this crossing of the Mokelumne by the diary of Padre Pedro Munoz. He was a priest in the expedition of Captain Gabriel Moraga. Moraga, with Sergeant Pedro Amador as second in command, and thirty-four of the *Soldados de Cuera* made the crossing of the river in the month of September in the year 1812. This in the course of his explorations for the Crown of Spain.

The Padre refers to the mesas on both sides of the stream and the enormous number of human skulls scattered along the banks, evidence of a fierce encounter between the local Miwok and the Washoe who came from over the Sierra in the autumn, to take the King salmon that swarmed upstream. The Padre says the water was black with their bodies. This has the sound of a tall tale. However in the mid nineteen-forties at the same place I have personally seen the same thing in the month of September. So we may well believe the Padre.

In the expedition's report the river, by reason of the macabre finding, was titled *"El Rio de las Calaveras."* Copies were made upon parchment and sent by dispatch rider down the thousand mile Camino del Rey from Old Monterey to Loreto, from there by ship to San Blas, across the Mar Vermejo and over the mountains to Mexico City. Soon copies were extant at the Torre del Oro in Seville and in the offices of the Council of the Indies at Torres.

For reasons that do not seem to be capable of explanation, the Americans shifted the name to the next river south. The larger stream was then given the name used by the adjacent Miwok, Mokelumne. They and the river are so labelled by John Sutter. Out of all of this comes the name of our sister county to the south, "Calaveras."

On the littoral between the growing town and the river was Poverty Bar, worked at a fever pitch by all who could crowd in and stake a claim. Widely varying estimates have been made of the millions and scores of millions in placer gold that was recovered. It is doubtful that a richer area of its size ever existed in California or anywhere else.

At the approximate center of the town there is an obtuse truncated cone of a waterworn stone of a dark green shade in sharp contrast to the surrounding grayish material. It was the cork on a literal gold mine. Upon the word of people who worked upon the dredger at that time; the buckets hit this stone at around sixty feet. There was then effected a close approximation of a break into Fort Knox. Gold came up in cubic foot dimensions to clog the trammels and conveyors, causing the motors to be stopped while crow bars were employed to loosen it from the machinery. Some pieces of it being of a size that could not be lifted by two men. By all accounts that day's take was several hundred thousand dollars.

While we are on the subject of alluvial gold deposits it is no exaggeration to state that there are at least a hundred miles of tunnels, drifts, stopes, and raises under the waters of Camanche Lake. At the destruction of the town miles of drifts were flooded, whole walls, ceilings, and floors sluiced across the dredger plates to leave gold literally measured by the millions. Posts, timber sets, and lagging littered the cobblestones.

In the fifties and sixties of the last century a type of mining was practiced in the area that was very high in yield and even higher in hazard. In the bluffs and barrancas close to the water's edge there were seams of rich gravel and coarse sand two to three feet in depth and exposed at the side where the river had deepened its channel. Spanish speaking persons long on nerve and short on prudence would form a team and work these deposits. Alternately one would lie upon his back and

8

excavate sideways, filling a rawhide *bota* with the pay dirt. His companion would drag this to the water's edge and wash it. The shallow ledges were rich, there was no outlay for digging drifts or timbering. The returns were great. There was just one revolting feature. Very frequently the whole dug-out would collapse upon the luckless miner. Not even funeral expenses were incurred, since to get the body out was a practical impossibility. This technique was termed *"como tejon o tejonero,"* (badger mining that is).

The immediate environs of *Lancha Plana* probably hold the best examples of the three basic techniques of placer mining that are visible from one observation point. On the benches on Chaparral Hill may be seen the rather small mounds of rock that were left in the wake of the sluice boxes and long toms.

Areas of cliff and bluff exposed above water line more particularly on the Calaveras side show the rhomboidal pattern of the terrain from which the pay strata has been removed by the monitors of hydraulic mining. The action of these monitors is just simply not to be believed. It is a chilling and numbing sight to watch cubes of earth the size of a house cut and quartered like cake by the two inch stream from the muzzle of the monitor. The blocked out material is disintegrated in a direct blast of the stream and the whole mass tumbles into the sluices where the gold is entrapped in the riffles. It is most awesome to watch its power demonstrated by passing a two by twelve-inch plank in front of the nozzle; the plank is cut as if by a saw. Let us not contemplate what happens to a human limb or torso thus exposed. And such has occurred in times past too.

The dredges that worked the river bed and banks from Camanche down toward the main dam left miles of giant cobbles brought up from bedrock. They were deposited in the characteristic windrow pattern that is the mark of the multi-ton buckets. This aggregate was eventually taken by earth movers and used to face the inner and outer slopes of the dam. And so from destruction came something useful.

May we for a moment digress to state that probably the best example of hydraulic mining's utterly destructive force may be seen on U. S. 80 above Dutch Flat in the area of Blue Canyon and Gold Run. Whole mountains just disappeared. They filled the bed of the Sacramento: —from a depth of thirty feet navigable by ocean going craft to a depth of ten feet: The detritus clogged two river channels, Suisun Bay, San Pablo Bay, and the Bay of San Francisco. It deposited the bar of the Potato Patch; offshore from the Golden Gate, then and now a permanent menace to navigation. Oh yes, the door was securely locked after the last nag had departed.

If anyone cares to see what gold dredges do there are miles and miles of boulder in the windrow pattern in the area of the Natomas north-east of Sacramento. They are as productive and useful as the landscape of the moon. The good earth that once nurtured orchards and alfalfa fields is fifty feet under.

And now to return to our city. In the usual pattern of the very early explosive growth of a mining community there was fire following fire until the inhabitants turned for building material to stone, both cut and field, adobe, tapia, and burned brick in the manner sketched in the prologue. *Tienda, Cantina, Panaderia,* and *Casa de Baile* now were properly housed. The ever present menace of fire was contained by ceilings supported by heavy timbers boarded over and covered with earth to a depth of perhaps six inches. The rafters, sheeting, and sugar pine shakes above could be replaced from the surrounding woodland if they fell a prey to the flames . . . as frequently they did.

By the mid 1850's Lancha Plana's streets were lined with masonry structures housing mercantile firms famous in the history of the West. The offices of the Butterfield Stage, Wells Fargo, Adams Express. The trading ventures of Captain Weber and Sam Brannan, banks and branch offices of New York and Boston firms.

At closing the clang of the great iron doors and shutters and the rasp of the locking bars rang out as the establishments were secured for the night against thievery, banditry, and most important, the ever present menace of fire.

A stout city drawing not weakness but strength from many races and cultures in the manner of the Mother Lode and of all California to this day. Italian veterans of Garibaldi's armies of liberation, tightlipped Yankees from the Grand Banks, bush lopers and trappers of the Hudson Bay Company, mountain men from the High Rockies, deserting seamen from Her Majesty's Navy, Spanish Californians, *Kes-kee-dees*, Frenchmen mostly for some reason from the Cote d'Or, Germans from the Rhineland, Kanakas up from the domains of King Kamehameha III and Kamehameha IV, Bascos from Bilbao, Portuguese from the Douro and Ponte Delgado in the Azores, Irishmen, Kildare, Kerry, and Waterford mostly in evidence, Missourians, well shaken in the jolting prairie schooners on the long road over the plains, Rockies, and the Sierra from Pike County. Spanish miners out of the Old Almaden and the silver workings of Guadalcanal, wind tanned Texans, the most skillful of all placeros, miners of Arispe and Hermosillo in Sonora, Georgians and Tarheels of North Carolina bringing the techniques of the rocker and the long tom from the gold fields of Dahlonega, Chinese in workaday garb of blue trousers, wide coolie hat, shirt outside of belt, and flapslapping slippers, Sunday and fiesta time in blue Mandarin cap, brocaded silk surcoat and high padded Mongolian boots, Chilenos off the tall ships clearing from Antofagasta. The powerful frames and oakline torsos of the local Miwok, bearded Mormons from the Mormon Battalion of the Army of General Stephen Kear-

11

ney, Peruvians hailing from Lima and Callao, Colombians out of Cartagena and Santa Fe de Bogota. Now curiously the silver coins of the last two named had a way of turning up in the sluice boxes in the area as late as the 1930's and 40's. About the size of a fifty cent piece or a trifle larger bearing on the obverse the statue of the Great Liberator and titled most appropriately, Un Bolivar.

In what previous time and when again will such a tapestry be woven?

As the roads opened and improved the *cargadores* and *arrieros* of the long mule trains pushed their wares to the higher camps and were replaced by the great freight wagons jolting out from Captain Weber's now grown up City of Stockton to the larger towns behind the long jerk line teams in cadence to the tuned Swiss Bells on the lead mules; the hard material of sophistication and civilization aboard; massive furniture of walnut and mahogany, king size beds, great carved chests, grand pianos with ebony shells, one such surviving until its destruction by fire in the roaring twenties. One magnificient piece may be seen from this era, a carved hardwood bar in the tavern of Fred Lyons at Burson, moved to this point from Camanche before its demolition and inundation.

The city directory of 1854 a priceless thing surviving lists the livery stables, booteries, harness and saddle shops, mortuarys, gunsmiths, gold dealers, bakeries, ladies' wear, tailor shops, watchmakers, jewelry stores, hardware, miners' supplies, physicians and surgeons, dentists, veterinaries, mercantile establishments of every conceivable type including one charming item from many here not listed: a studio dispensing lessons in piano, violin, and guitar.

Paralleling documents exist in an old daguerrotype, a copy being displayed in the offices of the East Bay Municipal Utility District in the City of Lodi. There is

12

no clue to its date, the best guess would probably place it in the mid-fifties.

It is taken from the upper end of Broadway. In the far distance there is no evidence of Union Bar or Put's Bar. A great fire in those mid-fifties obliterated them. This might help in pinpointing the date. The mesas on the south bank over in Calaveras are exactly as they appear now. The bold promontory of Alum Peak at the right and the rim rock running south-west from it might well have been photographed today. There is one difference. A hill in line with Alum Peak at the upper right and bearing north-east from it is simply not there now. Its site at present is marked by piles of stone. Evidently it was blasted to pieces by the monitors. It is most likely strewn in the streambed between there and the Potato Patch. On the bluffs at the rear there are several terminals of the Lancaster Ditch. Their height gave the required pressures in the penstocks for the operation.

May we now have a word upon the life blood of Lancha Plana—the water brought in by the Lancaster nourishing its placers and also supplying Camp O'pera, French Camp, Camp Union. At the Boston Store a spur wound interminable miles to China Gulch. It forked at the head to supply both sides and continued to Union Bar, Put's Bar and others lost to history. Finally it crossed the river to placers on the Calaveras side. Apparently it arrived there by a flume of tremendous size that has long since disappeared. In the old pictures of the diggings—a good example being Volcano in the 1850's—the flumes appear crossing each other at four or five different levels in exactly the same manner as the Los Angeles freeways downtown.

This Lancaster Ditch takes its beginning out of Jackson Creek. It courses around the base of mountains, through dug slots in the hills, by flume across the canyons. In its main course and branches thirty seven miles are logged. It was started in 1850, brought to completion in February of 1853. The miners who constructed it contributed sweat and took their pay in water script at the placers. The record of that time informs us that they were well paid. It is chronicled that this arrangement, while by no means universal was widely practiced in those days.

No estimate will ever be possible of the thousands of miles of mining ditches that were dug to bring water for the recovery of gold. How many times in climbing a mountain or canyon side in the Mother Lode does one come upon a ditch and, higher, another ditch? It is puzzling until one remembers that across the canyon behind the screen of the forest there is the other end and that a connecting flume once thrust its slender timbered frame down to the bottom of the gorge.

Out of the masonry buildings long departed of Old Lancha Plana one survives to this day. The old stone store at Buena Vista. In the year 1870 certain Chinese of Lancha Plana closed a real estate deal that for some strange features and bizarre qualities is something even in California the home of the strange real estate deal.

One William Cook of Buena Vista made a contract with a Tong of Lancha Plana. The name of the Tong remains back in the mists. It could have been the Hop Sings who threw plenty of weight at that time in that area. The deal was to dismember the building at Lancha Plana and move it to Buena Vista a distance of five statute miles. There to re-erect it, roof it and turn it over to the owner in operational condition as a mercantile establishment. The consideration: the privilege of mining the ground formerly occupied by the building. Accounts that have come down to us say they were well compensated for their labors.

Now, when we say, *moved,* an explanation is in order as to how. The moving was accomplished by long gin poles with enough shoulders under each end to lift and transport. The building is 30 feet wide, 72 feet long, 14 feet high at the plates and the walls are two and one half feet in thickness. Many individual stones in the walls are of several tons weight. Impossible. Of course, but there it is to this day.

One calls to mind Charles Crocker's discussion with Leland Stanford anent the hiring of the Chinese for the construction of the Central Pacific Railroad. Stanford was doubtful that the Chinese light of body structure and spare of frame could endure such rigorous tasks. Said Charles Crocker, "Well they built the Great Wall didn't they"? In all of the history of the West there is no more thrilling story than that of how Cholly Clocka and the China Boys pushed the rails of the Old Central Pacific around the promontory of Cape Horn, up into the Donner Pass, and over the Sierra.

The store moving operation was witnessed by several persons who survived until well into the 1940's. Their vivid imagery in describing it was unfortunately not tape recorded.

I asked James Fitzsimmons one of those who observed the reconstruction. Was there not great activity and much Cantonese heard around here "You just would not believe it if I told you," said James. "But it sort of gave you the feeling of looking at a giant ant hill into which someone had just poked a spade."

The timbers overhead supporting the ceiling are three inches by eighteen inches by thirty feet.

Here there enters a story that is entirely apocryphal. That these timbers were cut in the State of Maine, brought around the Horn by clipper, loaded upon a river steamer in San Francisco and transported upriver to Lancha Plana.

In the 1850's and 60's regular passenger and freight service was maintained to the *embarcadero* at Lockford. It is not inconceivable that in a time of high water the

15

fifteen miles above Lockford could have been negotiated. We must remember that in those earlier days the hydraulic operations had not silted up the stream.

The contemporary steamboatmen took cargoes upstream to incredible distances. Their vessels, loaded, drawing less than two feet of water. They used winches in their bows powered by engines. They attached cables to trees on the banks above the rapids and hauled themselves up in a manner somewhat resembling the bootstrap lift.

Two excellent examples of this type of craft were the steamers *Red Bluff* and *Dover* so equipped and operated on the upper Sacramento to Colusa and Red Bluff until the early 1930's. Their draft, fully loaded, with seven hundred tons of freight, was 22 inches. Yes, the story may well have been true. However, if one may be permitted a conjecture, it would be this: that the timbers in the building probably arrived as noted above, but that the ones in the rebuilt structure were obtained from some mill within a distance that did not present too much of a problem on transportation. The sawmill in Jackass Gulch may well have been the supplier as it is within a ten mile radius and the material could have been floated down Jackson Creek at high water. The timbers bear the mark of a circle saw and appear to be in substance California ponderosa pine.

In the hall of records in Jackson at the County Court House there is, in the map section, one of the city layout of Lancha Plana. These maps are all approximately five by eight feet. This one bears the date "1866." Southeast, facing the river, is the enclosure of Chinatown. Under the caption there appears the notation "Titles uncertain." An understatement of colossal proportions. Which we shall proceed to examine.

Under what appears to be a Cantonese practice a number of Chinese would form a group or association and purchase a fifty foot lot. In accordance with their theory the lot would be divided into five ten foot lots in frontage. This would seem to be somewhat of an abstraction further complicated by the probability that three persons might own one of the ten foot sections, seven another, and an undetermined number holding an aliquot title to the remaining portions.

Quite possibly upon the addition of a second story it would be leased, to give an example, by the Tong of the Suey Sings to that of the Bing Hong.

Comes now the County Assessor knocking at the door demanding the property taxes due the county. There follows an animated conversation between the several spokesmen on the behalf of the Orientals, pretending to much less knowledge of English than was theirs, and the assessor. In the background—heated exchange of words by the occupants in sibilant Cantonese of the dialect of She Pan as to who owed how much of which. A call next day and days afterwards by officialdom yielding less results. How many County Assessors, Tax Collectors, and their assistants succumbed to diseases of the vascular system, strokes, coronaries, and the like will never be known. They did finally arrive at an operational solution. "Leave em alone."

Past the 1870's the placers were in the era of diminishing returns. In the 70's hydraulic mining was outlawed after its staggering damages had been inflicted. The dredges did not appear until the early twentieth century. In the interim an exodus of thousands of miners. They were replaced by a few patient Chinese, content to scrape the gleanings in the gulches and arroyos:—enough to keep them in long grained China rice, dried squid, fragrant China Tea, and other necessities beloved of the natives of Cathay.

The Hispanic element, even in later days remained dominant right up to the final abandonment—the dynamiting of the old stone buildings, and the gutting of the townsite under the buckets of the giant dredge.

Mayhap, at this point a word or two upon costume may not be out of place. At picnic or fiesta ancestral garb would appear from its long repose in *armario,* camphor or cedar chest.

In 1910 while riding the pony to the picnic at Ione the writer was joined by five *caballeros* not in the habiliments of ordinary folk but fully turned out as *gente de razon.* The cloaks, enormous of size of broadcloth, either deep blue or the more numerous the black of a raven's wing. Their collars high chokers latched at the throat in the manner of the tunics of the Royal Canadian Mounted of today. Slits were placed in front at right and left through which the arms could be passed to control the mount. The linings, silk, in the colors of scarlet, turquoise, or lemon yellow.

The hats, beavers, flat crowned, medium of brim, black, very much in the pattern shown in a hundred TV or movie scenes portraying Spaniards in full dress. One excellent example survives in the show case at the Old Buena Vista Store, donated by Sarah Fitzsimmons. By her statement it belonged to Don Antonio Coronel, a friend of her father, founder of the Pueblo of Sonoma in Mexican times and of the town of San Andreas in the American era. He was a Spanish nobleman, Companion of the Order of the Knights of Malta, likewise of the Order of St. James of Compostella, Companion of the Order of the Golden Fleece. Higher than this order in Spain one does not go. His accumulation of titles may be verified in the published works of the state papers of Jose Figueroa, one of the governors of California in the middle Mexican period.

The shirts were of silk, with wide cuffs double buttoned, ruffled at the throat, snow white, cream, apple green, or the blue of a robin's egg.

The small vests or bolero jackets: gray, appearing to be of a thin felt, elaborately embroidered with silver thread, or an alternate pattern, black, worked with gold thread in the manner of the above.

The trousers, blue serge or black, split at bootside level showing a flash of scarlet, deep yellow, or cerulean blue silk.

The belts of tooled polychromed leather, wide to perhaps three inches, held by buckles of enameled and gold inlaid silver out of the shops of the Vermejos of Toledo.

Sashes with **pompons** and tassels of all shades of brilliantly colored silk. An example may be seen in the museum at San Andreas, protected by triple glass. It was taken from the body of Joaquin Murrieta after his death at the hands of the California Rangers at the Arroyo Cantova in July 1853.

The boots were high of heel, with toe pointed and squared, very much like the pattern used today. Quite probably our current designs are age old in heritage. These were black and polished to the brightness of a mirror.

In contrast to the black, silver-plated saddles and palomino mounts of the ranchos of the coastal area, the local preference in saddles seemed to run to a shade of tanning that we will attempt to describe as between a sherry wine and an old rose, most elaborately tooled and polychromed with gold leaf applied at points of emphasis.

Bridles with the Toledo work on the Spanish bits were common to both. Tension on the featherlight reins was maintained by silver chains crossing under the jaw, the reins terminating in a *romal*. Take note at any parade today, when the Californios, both Hispanic and Anglo, show their horseflesh. The basic designs have not changed.

In mounts as mentioned above the taste was for coal black, of an animal somewhat chunky in body, wide of forehead with great nostrils flashing red in moments of great excitement, slender of limb with small hoofs and long pasterns. In his heart the hot flame of Araby.

In the above is an attempt to sketch the tack and mounting of our Latin friends as they rode out of Old Lancha Plana on a Sunday morning to a picnic. In their company, our boy on a sorrel pony had all of the reactions of a sparrow who had fallen in company with a covey of birds of paradise.

Today the Spanish towns are in decline and decadence. Upon the whole earth, nothing is more haunting and inspiring of nostaglia. Crumbling balconies and ramadas are covered with bouganvillea and passifloria. An old California round-tailed center-fire saddle swings from a cross beam. Out at the corner a red pear olla of tremendous size—the water is of a coldness not to be believed—gourd dipper attached by a thong of rawhide.

The gold of ears of corn and the flaming scarlet of peppers at the doorways against cream plastered walls. Mexican *metates* and Miwok *morteros* are under the oleanders. The latter frequently contain water for the convenience of the family dog. At the side or rear the whited dome of the horno, dispensing on baking day, sour Latin bread and pastries of a deliciousness past belief. The measured sonorous tones of Spanish, the most beautiful of all of the tongues of man.

Fortune favors all of mankind in varying degrees. One piece of this fortune, incredibly good, is at the age of nine to have heard two guitars in the cadence of Al Caputin and La Golondrina floating out from the grid in a massive wall; a quartering moon in the backdrop.

California may attain to great power and influence in the world. With all of this she will be poverty stricken and miserably poor when from her soil has departed the last of the fire and ice of la Madre Espana.

Now if our ghost town under the waves is to be peopled with wraiths and sheeted forms in the elfish and inimitable style of Jo Mora's maps should we perhaps equip them with the scales and tails of mermaids and mermen? Our simile may well be entirely wrong. How about aqualungs? Now to you boatmen on Camanche Lake. Get out your chart or map. Draw a rhumb line from the buzzards cave on Alum Peak to the corner of the great mass of sandstone on the cliff south east over in Calaveras. Now please another from the tall digger pine on Chaparral Hill to the slot between the mesas back of old Union Bar. Run down either to its intersection with the other. You are now directly above La Panaderia, operated by La Molinera; girl friend and betrayer of Joaquin Murrieta. *Buena suerte e buen pescando.*

Camp Union

Let us now surface from the watery environs of Lancha Plana and move upstream a distance of perhaps a mile and a half to the first ravine bearing due north into Amador. An acceptable guess would be that a half mile up this ravine would be quite close to the center of the townsite.

On the hillside to the east there remain several chimneys, partly fallen, of large dimensions and several building foundations all of these in material being the native stone, a brownish rhomboidal substance apparently grouping with the serpentines or slates.

The bottom of the ravine is presently occupied by two dams, partially supplied by the local runoff during the rains but mainly using the Lancaster Ditch to fill to brim in the Spring.

In the course of the construction of the lower of the two dams there was bladed out a two story adobe, It was open to the sky, roofless, destitute of a second floor, patches of plaster still adhering to both inner and outer wall. In the window openings of the second story *nopale* cactus was growing in a manner exactly like that of pictures portraying the same in the outskirts of the Mexican City of Cherubusco.

Upon hearing that the old structure was to be razed I purchased color film to have proof that had existed. Arrival at the site was just twenty four hours late. It would have been a perfect color frontispiece for this book. How many times have documentary and artifacts been saved by fortunately falling to the other side of the razor's edge?

Was it perhaps a hotel, the town hall, armory and arsenal for the true blue Union Guards? The chances of our ever knowing are faint indeed.

French Camp

If we make perhaps three quarters of a mile of northing from the locale of the vanished adobe and travel in the same ravine we will be at center of French Camp. Here it is evident that much more has survived and the ruins cover a much wider area.

Huge chimneys still standing to a height of four or five feet dot the landscape. Stone walled enclosures that were once houses thrust their way up to three to five feet above grade.

Centering the ruins in a small flat at the bottom of the ravine is a stone structure, the purpose of which it is difficult to determine. It is square. The stones have been cut to present a smooth surface outward. In dimensions it is, at a guess, twenty feet on each face. It rises above grade level to a height of approximately five feet. No trace whatever exists of any window or door opening or indeed of any aperture whatever. Its interior is filled with earth which rises higher than the surrounding walls. The elements have eroded it to an angle of retention which leaves the center three or four feet higher than the perimeter.

To guess the purpose we may perhaps make headway if we associate it or even integrate it with a building that formerly stood immediately to the north. This was a handsome two-story edifice of burned brick; said, by the older people thereabouts, to have once been a bank. This theory is well supported—at ground level there was a very large safe, the door wide open around. We played there when quite small.

Just possibly this stone work at the rear might have housed individual storage vaults, access being had from the floor above. We had not done too badly thus far. But how do we account for its being filled with earth?

Here now is presented a quite logical question. In all of these references to brick structures how come there is not a scrap of one surviving?

Quite simply really. At a date beginning about forty years ago their dismemberment started. They were all coursed in lime mortar. This permitted the buildings to be taken apart with ease. The lime cleaned from the brick readily. They then became beautiful building blocks for walks, barbecue pits, garden walls and innumerable landscape projects.

As late as the early nineteen forties, Olde Muletown, to jump ahead a bit, contained twenty or thirty old brick chimneys and houses. Not a scrap or vestige of any of these remains, not even one brickbat.

If any brick structure whatever survives in a ghost town in the Mother Lode—and I do not know of any such

—there will be found in close proximity a citizen with a twelve gauge in fine serviceable condition. The said citizen being obdurate of temperament will have the will, at need, to do his simple duty. So far the two-legged pack rats have scored a one-hundred per cent victory. This now may well be an evaluation that is entirely too harsh. The bricks were—and if any are still obtainable—tempting to an unbelievable degree. The old hand molds and more than a century of erosion gave them a texture that nothing around can even approximate. For their color—to envision it mentally—try throwing upon the palette a bunch of fireweed, a stick of cinnamon, and a dab of Chinese vermillion. To resist these one must be entirely unresponsive to color, or possessed of a lofty ethical nature. I am uncertain as to how many of us might pass the test.

French Camp deserves to be noted for its preëminence in having two *hornos* or ovens of the type mentioned in the prologue. The larger, under an oak tree could be put into operation with about thirty minutes of work on the door arch. The other, as of this writing is in perfect shape and useable for a barbecue. The lime plaster encasing both has long since eroded. Not a trace remains.

W. D. Mason states that the earliest inhabitants of French Camp were mainly Gallic in origin. Which neatly disposes of the name applied. He further states that subsequently the population was mixed—in very much the pattern of the other camps.

The late Frank Fish in the year before his passing expressed much interest in visiting French Camp. This was arranged. As a prelude to his activation of his electronic exploration equipment, he went way out on a limb with this flat statement. "In all of my years afield I have never in a days' operation failed to turn up an artifact that is not worthy of display in my museum. It may not be a coin or any precious metal but it will be a thing of archaeological value." After thus cornering himself, he got, within perhaps five minutes, a buzz on the metal detector. Excavation turned out an axe head of a pattern unknown in these parts. He called it, and, later, in one of his text books, proved, that it was Spanish and eighteenth century.

The haft was formed by welding the metal around a form instead of being molded as is the current and long time practice. It was displayed in his museum in Amador City forthwith.

Subsequent to his departure his priceless collection appears to have been strewn to the winds, and of course so went the axe.

Camp O'pera

Here with Camp O'pera there is posed a question or mayhap a mystery concerning its spelling. Contemporary references to it spell it Camp Opra. It is thus spelled in mention of it in an issue of *Holiday* Magazine of sometime back. The older records however give it unanimously as Camp O'pera. Neither English or Spanish orthography would seem to account for this horsecfeather of an apostrophe riding high between the capital O and the lower case p. But there it is so let us see what we can do with it.

Such fragments as may be recovered and assembled of its earliest period seem to agree that in the summer of 1849 forty or fifty Sonorian miners were dry washing with *bateas* and getting a fair return of coarse gold. The account parallels that which may be discovered at this time if one engages in washing operations during the Winter rains in the little creek that runs by the townsite edge. The gold you get is of a faintly violet shade and is no larger and no smaller than a grain of wheat.

Now, for a moment, this thing of the color of gold. If you will observe closely no two gold coins are of exactly the same shade unless they come from the same area.

For instance the gold from certain locations of the Trinity is of a deep almost a blood red hue. In the vicinity of Rescue in El Dorado County less than five miles from Coloma, where Jim Marshall started the big scramble, the gold is an unearthly green.The coinage from the great depths of the Argonaut and Kennedy Mines shades toward red with a slight tinge of purple. I have seen doubloons from the mint at Cartagena that were of a shade of butter. Now this is true even after the metal has been alloyed with copper to the standard 90 - 10 of coinage. The color variations are not due to impurities. They are intrinsic in the pure element *Au*.

Until the Government closure of the mines in the early 1940's the personnel at the San Francisco Mint and at the Selby Smelting and Refining Company in the Transbay could pinpoint to within a mile and a half of the point of origin of any gold—by the color test mainly. Sluice box robbers, claim jumpers, and all kinds of illegal operations were by this fact uncovered and brought to an accounting with the law.

Now to return to the main line. No very large addition to the population seems to have occurred until the Isaac's Ditch brought water to the placers in 1851. The count seems to have gone up to several hundred.

The push to the final population peak came with the arrival of the Lancaster Ditch. This, for long stretches, paralleled the Isaac's at a level 30 feet higher. This brought water, under increased pressure, to the hills back of the town.

Operations in Black Gulch, or Arroyo Negro, if you prefer the Spanish, were multiplied many times. In turn the population rose to an estimated two or three thousand. It was somewhere in this bracket when Juan Sanchez a member of Joaquin Murrieta's band was taken out of the Grand Palace Saloon and hung by Sheriff Clark's posse on Feb. 23, 1853. Where the hang tree stood we will never know. It may have been one of the great oaks still standing. As late as twenty years ago there were people alive who could tell, but were not asked.

The old accounts tell that it was a town of twenty buildings and that twelve of those buildings were saloons. One cannot help but wonder what mundane purposes the other eight structures served. Could they have been stores, livery stables, warehouses? One small segment of this question we answered years back when with a metal detector we dimensioned out a blacksmith shop of perhaps 25 x 50 feet directly across the little stream from the town well. It is highly improbable that any of these eight structures were used as private dwellings, at least not in the earlier phases.

The story comes down to us that in the olden time the place was notorious for its graveyard of drunks, that the cemetery was the last resting place for those who died of delirium tremens. Its location is known to very few at this time. It is an approximate mile to the west of the townsite, the terrain gently rolling, and studded with great oaks. Any connecting road has long since disappeared.

An aerial photo of the date of 1946 may be examined to locate many of the individual interments with fair precision. Unfortunately in the intervening time the ground has been plowed which makes individual identification difficult if not impossible.

Before her passing twenty years ago I asked Sarah Fitzsimmons—she then being in her nineties—if she could give with some information upon the drunks' graveyard. I do not believe that I have ever before seen an aged person so angry. This is her quote: "That was the last resting place of many a decent and honorable citizen, some of them known to me personally. It is true that in the beginning it sheltered some alcoholics, and what place of burial doesn't?" The statement is not a half-truth, it is not even a one-tenth truth. A perfect example of the garbling and distortion that is so often passed off for history.

Until forty years ago or thereabouts the one remaining piece of evidence of it once being a place of interment was a bricked-up plot enclosure. We have accounted for the disappearance of the brick in our bit on French Camp. No evidence remains whatever of the original purpose to which the field was placed. A word upon the owner of the former bricked-up enclosure. Upon the word of James Moore, William Nichols, and Richard Barnett it was one Painter. This seems to have been anglicized from Pintor. Anyway it adds up to Painter in both languages.

It was he who planted the black mission fig trees that still grow along the bank of the stream and the yellow nopale cactus that grew in profusion until destroyed by the great freeze of some years back. In the deep trench of Cactus Gulch it grew solid, bank to bank.

Now an aside: All through the Mother Lode one may follow the trails left by the Mexicans by what they planted—the Nopale Cactus and the Black Mission Fig. The cactus was sweet fruit in season and green vegetable; vitamin C for salad the twelve-month around. The Black Mission Fig was heavy with fruit in June and again with the second crop in September. When dried it was absolute tops as a confection and as iron rations on pack saddle, in saddle bags, or even in any available space in a pocket.

From a source now utterly lost, Padre Ugarte brought the black fig to the Mission of San Jose Commondu in Baja California in the year 1747. From Commondu it

28

was taken to all of the missions of Alta California. In the influx of people from below the border, scions were picked up at the missions, brought to the Lode and planted—to the great good fortune of those of us who came by later. Padre Ugarte said that the Mission Fig would enrich the Californias for the next thousand years. So it was and so it shall be.

Upon the south slope of a hill of deep black soil, once a part of the old ranch and still called by the old timers, the Painter Place, he raised vegetables, berries, and fruit. He sold to the miners and gave to them when they were broke or in hard circumstances. A true benefactor of mankind.

For many years the gateposts of his long vanished home stood, in springtime and summer, in a glorious mass of the old stickery Blass Moss Roses beloved of the Forty Niners. By the long gone right hand post there still stands a tall oak supporting a large grape vine which he planted. In the month of September it is loaded with eighteen inch long clusters of the Almeria or Red Malaga, tasty beyond belief.

Since all communities must have an economic base let us examine for a moment the placer fields that nourished the town and kept the little balls clicking in the roulette wheels in the palaces of chance. Black Gulch, in its flanks and in places at the crest, has visibly been scoured out and eroded to a depth of many feet. To the immediate west of the building sites one half of a hill is missing. The remaining portion has the look of having been parted from the front section with a giant cleaver.

Now let us see if we cannot take several pieces of a jugsaw puzzle, fit them together, and form a picture. Within a half mile of the town, on the west there is, at present, a small water course. It is now active only during the Winter and Spring rains. On the old Spanish maps it is marked as *"Las Cienegas del Sur"* and shows a series of small lakes clear down to the confluence with

Jackson Creek. We will use the English term current hereabouts "the South Slough." One of these lakes, just east of Highway 88 is still there, exactly as the old maps show. It is almost a mile long, perhaps a hundred yards wide, ten to fifteen feet deep. Ample water to float both the Robert E. Lee and the Natchez.

Another piece of the puzzle: In the twenties a well was sunk, it was close to the upper part of the water course. At a depth of ninety feet the diggers struck what was obviously the town dump—bottles, crockery, and various bits of books and magazines, all in Spanish. Now we know what happened. The lakes were filled by the blast of the monitors with earth from the slopes above.

Now for some side effects: It is well documented that Jackson Valley, immediately to the west, supported the greatest concentration of an Indian population in all California. U. S. Gregory, in his memoirs, states that as late as 1870s there were five thousand Indians there resident.

Their base of subsistence was this. The valley was one giant orchard of mammouth oaks yielding acorns by uncounted tons which, after the elaborate processes applied by the Indians to remove the tannic acid, became good and nutritious food.

As was true along the Molelumne the King Salmon choked the waters of the South Slough, requiring only to be hauled out and kippered to fill the native storehouses with their dietetic requirement of protein for each season. Such an aboriginal elysium has had few if any duplications in history. Small wonder that the *kiva*, or dance house, now in ruins at the community of *Uu - poo - sun - e* was the largest in California.

And there was more. South and west of the valley there is a giant natural fortification; a plateau of rimrock several hundred acres in extent exhibiting almost all of the features of seventeenth and eighteenth century military defenses.

It is all there from the hand of nature, scarp, glacis, bastion, sally port, even an inner *enciente,* formed by two Buena Vista peaks and the cliffs surrounding them. The peaks function as watch towers for the whole system. Nothing seems to have been forgotten. In the saddle between the peaks there gushes forth a live stream of pure ice cold water. Thirst was never a problem.

How Sebastien Vauban would have loved it. There is not much that he could have added to it, really, since it was all there already.

The greater portion of the Indians' massive oaks were cut to make way for farming operations. The waters of the South Slough have disappeared beneath the detritus of the placers. Only a handful of Indians survive.

No attempt is here made to moralize, but suppose we note that the consequences of the American's wanton and casual destruction of anything human, animal, vegetable, or mineral that lies athwart of his pursuit of a buck is beginning to overtake him in these latter decades of the twentieth century.

We now approach the curtain on the final act on the old town. According to James Fitzsimmons, long after the last faro dealer and Mexican girl from the Casa de Baile had departed for greener fields, there remained two old Spaniards, Carlos and Julio. Their surnames are not of record. Jim was sure that they both were out of the Estremadura—that God-forsaken part of the Spanish Wild West that is below Madrid.

They were content to pan gold in the gulches for a return that kept them in bacon, beans, and blue jeans. After years, the infirmities of age removed Julio to the County Hospital and to his exit from a troubled world. Carlos carried on. Finally he was discovered to be missing, and, after an intensive search, his body was found up one of the canyons. In his cabin was found a cap box half filled with coarse gold, in value probably around two hundred dollars.

Henry Russell, the father of my friend Frank was a member of the group that discovered the body. In telling the story, he mentioned that Carlos' old musket was missing. Frank was a boy of twelve. This was many years after the event tried to conjecture where it might have been dropped before the end. His calculations proved to be correct. He found the ancient weapon atop a small hillock about two hundred yards distant.

The stock was worm eaten and mostly gone in the manner that Washington Irving tells of the piece belonging to Rip Van Winkle. I have seen it. It bears the stamp "Harper's Ferry Aresenal," and the date 1837.

Townerville

The genesis of Townerville appears later than most of its neighboring communities.With the outbreak of the Civil War copper became a resource that was possibly more precious than gold. Then, as now, copper and mercury were number one strategic metals in the chariot of Mars.

Mason relates of Townerville and Copper Center that they were ephemeral in character, a free translation of which would seem to be that they sprang into existence with the outbreak of the conflict. At its close the price of copper declined. The towns died.

Their site is beneath the waters of the north arm of Lake Pardee. When the lake is below normal levels, there is exposed the fallen walls of a building that was once part of the ranch house of the Horton holdings. The walls were overthrown by demolition crews in the course of the clean-up of the basin, to prevent them from being a menace to navigation. They were of serpentine, coursed in lime mortar. When standing, they would appear to have formed a combination of store and *bodega* or wine cellar.

In the long *chemise* covered hog-back of Bull Run Hill, back of the town were a number of kidneys of copper ore, extremely rich. By this is meant that the ore assayed 60% or 70% in metallic content.

Such scant information as is available seems to indicate that the ore was hauled by freight wagons over to the smelter of the Newton Copper Mine at Ranlett.

In the First World War several remaining kidneys were exploited and the known deposits of the ridge pretty well exhausted. There are persons surviving who mined the area and they remarked on the richness of the ore and on the rather unusual geologic formation—the ore bodies are isolated and completely unconnected by any copper bearing lode. The strikes were made at depths of from 150 to 300 feet.

Middle Bar

For a Sunday or week-end drive it is doubtful if there is existent a more pleasant excursion into ghost town land than that of crossing from South Jackson down the densely wooded canyon to the site of Middle Bar and, across the spidery steel cantilever of the old bridge spanning the Mokelumne, out into the narrow gulch. At roadside one is amazed at the massive masonry. It was obviously done in the 1850's or 60's, and subsequently supplemented by great billets and slabs of concrete of the surface works of the great Gwinn Mine.

The best time is in March or April when the almond, apple and quince trees are in bloom on the townsite.

They, a few abbreviated walls, and rectangular building footings are all that remain.

In dropping below the gradient of Highway 49 it is a most unexpected pleasure to enter a forest of the type that one encounters twenty miles to the east and three thousand feet higher.

Ponderosa, pepperwood, laurel, and black mountain oak of great size clothe the canyons and ridges. At the bottom a stream, vigorous even in Summer, finds its way out to the Mokelumne. Surely Sherwood Forest was not a greener nor more pleasant cover for the age old profession of banditry than the good green wood of Middle Bar. In the early 50's Joaquin Murrieta found its protective depth useful when he campaigned as the Robin Hood of El Dorado. In filling out the cast for Little John, Alan Adale, and Will Scarlett please write in Sevalio, Reyes Feliz, and Joaquin Valenzuela. In replacing the Sheriff of Nottingham, Clark of San Andreas will do nicely.

The road is narrow, the grade below dropping hundreds of feet to the gorge. If one meets another vehicle something in protocol has to be worked out as to who is best at backing for at least a half mile in places. Not recommended for timorous drivers but reasonably safe if care is exercised.

From the concrete footings of the Hardenburg hoists and gallows frames to the massive remains of the Gwinn, a distance of perhaps five miles, there is in view the Mariposa slate gouge piles and the foundations of the buildings of mine after mine. No small operations these —shafts of hundreds or thousands of feet in depth with batteries of stamps at the surface and employing hundreds of men at their peak of operations. Here we see the story that substantiates the old accounts. At a relatively early date, Middle Bar turned from the recovery of placer gold to engage in deep hard rock mining. A listing of the larger and more productive of these mines

34

would include the Nevills, Mc Kinney, Marlette, Sargent, Farrel, Julia, Meehan, St. Julien (very rich), Valparaiso, and Middle Bar.

Historians assert that at an early date the Middle Bar locale was predominately English in population. This would account for the deep hard rock claims. The Cousin Jacks from Penzance appear to have immediately turned to what for them was "doing what comes naturally."

Big Bar

At this site one is confronted with the difficulty of accounting for and endeavoring to reconcile a fact of terrain with what appears to be a fact of history. The chronicles of the early 50's are emphatic in assigning to Big Bar a population of over a thousand. Now the topography there is just about entirely vertical. The canyon slopes are quite close to qualifying as cliffs. Where the miners built their cabins and where some spot was turned into a small bit of a business district is certainly not visible at this time. Perhaps the inhabitants drove piling and spiles into the slopes and ascended from one level to another in somewhat the same manner as that used in a step pueblo of the Southwest.

Contemporary records of those 50's state that the recovery of alluvial gold by the use of wingdams was, even for that time, phenomenal. Which poses another large unanswered question. By what methods were the necessary materials brought to the site and how were they utilized after their arrival? Butte Canyon and Rattlesnake Creek, at present filled with a dense growth of ash and beech trees, appear to have had their beds scraped clean. In its lower course, Butte Canyon seems to have been stripped of thin veins of quartz that were probably rich. Diverting a stream that flowed vigorously all summer and was more in the nature of a fall than a rapids must have required considerable ingenuity—a faculty with which the miners of that time were well endowed.

Processing of the recovered quartz may have been effected by *arrastres* or *chile* mills but they were certainly not in the immediate area. There is no bit of ground level enough for an ore race on the mountain sides. The room required for an additional space for a tow path for the mules and the arc of the sweep is even more out of the question.

Until the early years of this century there remained primitive ore reduction facilities or rather the remains of them in the vicinity of the Zeile Mine. It may be that the pay portion was transported to them up Butte Canyon by pack train.

Old newspapers of the 50's recount numerous strikes made in Hundred Ounce Gulch.

Transporting the values down the gulch, down the river, and up the canyon must have been an arduous task. The present Highway 49 on the Calaveras side, after a number of re-alignments and the expenditure of great sums, is still a series of hairpin turns and tight circles. The Amador side is even more forbidding. A gallery has had to be blasted out of the greenstone wall of Butte Canyon, and at a very steep grade.

What communications might have been in the area a century ago and more would have had to be extremely sketchy. This may have been one of the trails that gave birth to a road sign much used by the '49-ers. "Road not entirely impassible just barely jackassable."

Quincy

All evidences of human habitation were removed from the site of Quincy more than a century ago. Writing his book in 1881, W. D. Mason stated as fact that there was absolutely no trace of a city in existence when he went to press. And he makes a curious observation which runs something like this: "How many plowmen down in Ione Valley, when they look up at the ridge north-east above them, know that they are gazing at the locale of a once prosperous town?" This topographic statement is entirely correct. The upland is visible from almost any part of the valley, and at the site, the fields below are suggestive of a great map unrolled away from one on the living room rug.

Some explanation is now in order as to why this obliteration of Quincy, Muletown, Live Oak, and other communities came to pass. These sites are all within the present boundaries of the Rancho Arroyo Seco locally referred to simply as, The Grant.

In 1841 Juan Bautista Alvarado then governor of California issued a grant of eleven square leagues of land to Teodosio Yorba. He was of the Yorbas of San Juan Capistrano. His grandfather helped Padres Barona and Suner and the architect Miguel Aguilar of Culiacan build the great Capistrano Mission. To this day, the Yorba family function as caretakers of the Mission to which the swallows always return on March 19—making the necessary corrections for leap year.

Yorba made no effort to occupy his land and in 1844 sold it to Andreas Pico; the consideration being five hundred head of longhorn cattle.

Andreas Pico was the brother of Don Pio Pico, the last Mexican Governor of California. Andreas was also the victor of the battle of San Pascual, when 87 of Los Galgos Californios inflicted a decisive defeat upon more than 300 of the Fifth Dragoons of the U. S. Army. If one cares to look, some of the lance heads of beautiful Toledo steel that were used in that operation may be viewed in the museum section at Mission San Miguel.

The original *diseno* or *derrotero* of The Grant is in the archives in the basement of the State Capitol at Sacramento. Both map and text are delineated upon a sheep's hide. A working replica is on file in the hall of records at the court house in Jackson. It is signed and attested by Juan Bautista Alvarado, verified and countersigned by Carlos Bustamente, then president of Mexico.

Pico made no attempt to use the Grant until after the American occupation. The incoming American settlers, thought that it was in the public domain, and built the City of Quincy. They were astounded and shocked when informed that they were trespassing upon private property and were served notice by emissaries of Pico to vacate the premises within a reasonable time. Pico was entirely within his rights. The treaty of Guadalupe Hidalgo, terminating hostilities between the United States and Mexico, specifically provided that all titles to land and property held under Spanish and Mexican sovereignty were valid under American law. To have asserted this in Quincy, in the time of trouble, would have been no recipe for longevity. The hatred endured until a generation ago, and is probably not yet extinct at this date. As a boy I remember the feelings held by older citizens. They were small children at the time of eviction and destruction. It was a hard physical thing of bitterness and animosity. Some were for armed and organized resistance. Others counseled moderation and an appeal to the Supreme Court for relief of a desperate situation.

There followed a dark period of several years, stained

by murder, ambuscade, and small scale guerilla warfare, the accounts of which are clouded and distorted by the intense partisan spirit of the participants. The above fits into California History under the heading of "The Great Squatters Riots of the Fifties."

One oldster I recall had a vivid recollection of both fear and admiration in watching the vaqueros from Mission San Jose maneuvering in perfect formation as a troop of cavalry in full dress and armament on the plain below and then riding into town like the wind at the back of Don Andreas. Now that the passions of a passed century have cooled it could be said of Pico that in another time he would have been worthy to have ridden at the right hand of Rodrigo Diaz against the Moors of Saragosa.

Local tradition says that sometime during this period of trial and tribulation, Pico's wife was murdered. Her grave is located—though at present unmarked—in a most beautiful setting in a little glen, surrounded by giant rock outcroppings and shaded by great oaks some six miles south of Quincy near the ruins of the great dance house of the Miwok town of *Uoo-poo-soo-ne*.

The Methodist Church in Ione, built of Muletown brick, designed by Thomas Mandell, and said to be the most perfect specimen of Gothic architecture for its size in the United States was foundationed and started in the early fifties. In the time of trouble work upon it was discontinued and not resumed for a period of more than ten years, or until after peace was restored.

To return to the conflict:—

A correct decision, at high level, was finally made and executed. From the Presidio of San Francisco a battalion of infantry, a battery of field artillery, and a troop of cavalry were dispatched to Ione Valley with orders to end bloodshed and strife. The site of their encampment is not now known, but some evidence would place it on the flat below Dutschke Hill, and within the afternoon shadow of the butte of Yerba Buena. Armed Federal forces garrisoned the area until well after 1865. In the intervening years the white flames of hatred were given a chance to cool to embers.

When the forces of reason resumed control, the settlers were offered the alternative of keeping Quincy and abandoning Ione or keeping Ione and abandoning Quincy. They elected to abandon Quincy for Ione and it was so consummated. Transfer titles were issued, from The Grant, to ownership in the Ione holdings. These are still the basis of property claims thereabouts.

By a decision of the Supreme Court under date of 1859 the south boundary of the rancho was moved north of the Mokelumne, the North boundary was moved south of the Cosumnes, the phrase, La Sierra Immurata (the inwalling Sierra) was determined to be the foot of the wall, as adjoining property owners maintained, and not the top of the wall (the crest of the Sierra), the position of the owners of the rancho. The west boundary, the Camino del Sacramento was fixed at some six miles west of the Sacramento County line.

This left a domain of some 78,000 acres. Sales and transfers of property in the City of Ione, Ione Valley, and Jackson Valley cut the acreage to somewhere around 58,000. It is presently owned by the Crocker Anglo National Bank or at any event is a portion of the Howard Estate, whatever its status may be. Permission to visit the site of Quincy would have to be obtained from the headquarters of the rancho on the old Stockton road south of Ione, though why anyone would desire to do so would be unclear; there is very little to see.

In the month of May 1963, a delegation of the County Historical Society, by permission of the management, went over the ground of the former town.

All the techniques of obliteration had not been sufficient to erase the great width of main street; good for four lanes of traffic with additional room for diagonal parking. The cross streets were also of generous dimensions. We counted twenty-seven filled-in wells, which probably constituted the town water supply. Several members of the Society brought photostatic copies of maps from the files of the *Quincy Prospect* in the State Library in Sacramento. An aerial photograph and these maps would probably be in almost complete agreement. Brush has not grown back in what were once traffic lanes and the grass cover is much shorter there than in the building lots.

From the maps and examination of the site we were able, with fair accuracy, to locate the position of Cunningham's store, the greatest emporium in miles around. For all practical purposes the store served as the southeast corner of Quincy and the north-west corner of Muletown. Cunningham was famed for his good deeds and many acts of kindness to those less fortunate. In other facets of his many-sided personality he performed the function of town wit and raconteur.

If we wish to have more upon Quincy we shall be forced to mine the files of the *Prospect*. Those issues in the closing days, relating to the claims of the owners of the Arroyo Seco. As a fire precautionary measure the newspaper should have been printed upon abestos.

Muletown

We southeast from Cunningham's store and we are in Muletown. On the irregular but gently sloping terrain it is at this date difficult to pick out or discern foundations or streets. Trees three feet in diameter have grown at random breaking the geometric pattern of a town either when viewed from the air or at ground level. As late as fifteen years ago numerous chimneys and footings or red Muletown brick still portrayed the grid pattern of the settlement. These have long since disappeared into walks, patio walls, and barbecue pits leaving no trace of their former position.

However the older buildings in the business district of Ione are all constructed of Muletown brick and for a long time we will be able to enjoy their soft iridescent reds. The location of the kilns that produced them, and, from the quantity of output, they must have been of considerable dimensions, is not known.

Both early and modern geologists note with considerable interest the peculiar character of the Muletown gravels. These have been smoothed and polished by marine action. Some authorities are of the opinion that the gravels originated in a tributary or spur of the great Blue Lead and subsequently were subjected to the action of the ocean. Whatever their origin they were very rich and yielded a high percentage of large nuggets. One Chinese, having found a nugget weighing 36 ounces Troy, departed immediately for Cathay. Undoubtedly a most wise decision. The life expectancy of a Chinese in the diggings in the 1850's was not great enough to warrant taking any additional risks.

In 1854 the Johnston Brothers brought in the ditch from Dry Creek. With water available under pressure, the placers entered their most productive period. This in turn swelled the population to its maximum. It has been stated that a return of one thousand dollars per week was by no means uncommon at the sluices when sufficient water was at hand. This is not comparable to the staggering richness of the Butler Claim at Put's Bar, but still quite respectable.

There does not seem to be at hand any ready explanation as to why the brick work of Muletown was spared when Quincy, Live Oak, and other communities were denuded to the bare earth. One possible answer could be that the McNealy Copper Mine at the back of the town was brought into production in the mid-fifties and that the ownership of The Grant had an interest in its development. Though long abandoned, there still remains ample evidence that McNealy was once a great mine. Its point of maximum production was doubtless during the Civil War. Historians have repeatedly told us that the gold of California and the silver of Nevada were crucial in deciding the outcome of that conflict. Let us add to this that the copper of the California mines and quicksilver from the New Almaden of Santa Clara were of no less weight.

The old writers comment upon the ungainly appearance and awkward motions of the local Irish inhabitants, of Muletown who, having purchased horses, rode forth on Sunday in search of fun and frolic. The sight of these horsemen, with flopping limbs and unsteady posture, brought forth the response, "Ah the Muletown crowd."

Live Oak

Until the late 1940's there stood at a present road intersection a two-story building, massive in its proportions of gray cut stone, and exhibiting a fine degree of architectural balance. Imbeciles and half-wits, in a stupid search for treasure, have collapsed the upper walls, torn the great second story floor joists from their keys in the walls and have brought the whole thing down in complete ruin. A few scraps of what, by stretching the imagination, can be labelled local tradition, assert that this building was once a stagecoach stop. This is so often said about any ruin that is still visible that we may not attach too much importance to it. Here the story could well end except for one fact.

In the years 1960 and 1961 the U.S. Geological Survey had a field party in the area doing a topographic map in ten foot contours to replace one of prior date showing fifty foot contours only. I was a member of that party.

We discovered four streets, faced on each side by the stubs of the walls of great stone buildings. The buildings themselves had been removed from the scene. The count of these, as I recall, was eighteen. A most thorough job had been accomplished, the wall remnants were at a minimum six inches above grade and at a maximum two feet. This of course was all done by horse power, four footed, that is. The cost must have been a thing to note.

Again we are driven to conjecture. The only possible answer seems to be that since the site is within the boundaries of the Rancho Arroyo Seco it suffered the fate of Quincy and other settlements. All traces of human occupancy, in as far as is possible to do so, were completely destroyed. Rome probably did not do any better job on Carthage.

Another unanswered question. Why was the two story structure spared the fate of its neighbors?

Let us now attempt an evaluation. It is elemental that a community possessing eighteen edifices of masonry in the downtown area was possessed of a population of some hundreds or thousands and was of some prestige and weight in the affairs of that day.

Now to the blank wall. No mention is made of it in the writings of Mason, Doble, Taylor, Borthwick, Robinson, or as far as can be determined by any scribe of that time. When the number of people postulated by the physical evidence thereabout is assembled in an area of that dimension for any considerable period of time historic events had to occur but we just do not have any record of them.

The name itself is not a thing of certainty. Several persons resident within a few miles of the site state that it was called Live Oak and some of them were not quite sure. Here together with many other puzzles is a fine subject for additional research.

Carbondale

Here, in sharp contrast to the foregoing, we have a level terrain, later development, and the exploitation of a different mineral. In the 1860's a substantial and determined effort was made to locate coal deposits to fuel California's infant industries. At Carbondale a brown lignite was discovered at a depth of seventy feet. These deposits are extensive and underlie a large portion of the clay and alluvium in both Ione and Jackson Valleys. At Dutschke Hill, a few miles distant, two seams, approximately five feet in thickness, are exposed. Excavation for a clay pit revealed their edges in a hundred foot depth.

Close examination of one of the seams exposed will reveal colossal redwood logs piled at random atop of each other. Bark, foliage, and small seed cones may be picked out of the mass; the bark and cones retaining their original brown color, the foliage in spots still of a greenish hue, all readily identifiable as the Sequoia Sempervirens now confined to the north coastal portions of California.

Shafts were pushed down to mine this material and subsequent to the extension of the railroad to Ione in the 1870's transportation was at hand and the coal was shipped from there over the sections of Northern California that were served by rail.

As a result the town grew and, quite understandably, was named Carbondale. This, most likely, from a touch of nostaglia on the part of the miners from Pennsylvania. This brown coal or lignite was quite satisfactory for furnaces used at that time to heat private homes and apartments. It was however somewhat deficient in BTUs for raising steam in locomotive and steamship boilers.

To serve this demand several companies at Carbondale installed machinery for making briquettes. These bricquettes, produced by extrusion at tremendous pressures, were a product that fulfilled the need for a uniform and entirely clean fuel, having the required heat content. They were widely used, both for power and for home heating. The town grew again, beyond its previous limits. It had an added assist from the fact of being in the center of a great expanse of cow country and being a rail head.

In 1911 there were three large warehouses on one side of the main street. On the other were a block of tall two-story wooden Victorian buildings with plank sidewalks, post-supported upper balconies, watering troughs and hitching racks in front. There were signs designating the usual hotel, general store, livery and feed stables, post office, Odd Fellows' Hall, etc. and swinging doors on the saloons. Any TV or movie company could have used it as a set for Dodge City or Deadwood with no alteration whatever.

In the gay nineties, California's booming and zooming oil production displaced coal as a fuel on the railroads, and in most operations in industry. This happened a full generation before the transition in Mid-continent and the East. The briquette producers were forced out of business. One, no doubt the most rugged and resourceful survived until 1916.

Passenger service was discontinued at the railway

station very early in this century. Freight was suspended in the twenties. The warehouses and the railway station were torn down. Until a few years back, a siding served several shacks of the maintenance crews. These are now gone. Somewhere in the intervening time the town disappeared. The Carbondale rural school vanished and the few, if any, that it might serve are bussed into Ione. A solitary house across Laguna Creek is now vacant and rapidly falling into ruin.

The old shafts north of town are identified by the gouge piles and pieces of machinery that once produced briquettes that are too heavy and cumbersome to be negotiated by the junkies. One thing remains: the pens, corrals, runways, and loading chutes for the cattle, still very much in use by the ranchers.

Ranlett

A rare case in point: A community based upon a mine possessing more lives than a cat. If everything documentary could be assembled and evaluated it would probably show that copper mining in the Mother Lode or for that matter in all of California owes more to W. D. Newton than to any other person. The mine at Ranlett bears his name and all data that can be located credits him with opening the original shaft. This at the time of the terrific demand pressed by the Civil War.

The files of the *Sacramento Bee* of Civil War date make repeated references to shipments of copper concentrates from the Newton to the water transportation at Stockton. Obviously, the material went by the only possible route at that time; Cape Horn to smelters on the East Coast.

47

The output of Newton, Townerville, Copper Center, Muletown, Copper Hill and others that did not get to the notice of history appears to have been concentrated at some point on the road below Ranlett and hauled in the lumbering freight wagons to Captain Weber's *embarcadero.*

The close of hostilities seems not to have generated enough fall in price to have resulted in suspension of the operations.

Mason gives, in considerable detail, the processes used in producing the concentrates and remarks casually (date 1881) that production had continued since the war. His assertion that the product was sent to Swansea (he apparently can only mean Swansea in Wales) must presuppose that the concentrates were high in metallic content and high enough in value to justify transportation that incredible distance by sailing ship.

Between the time that his monumental work was printed and the close of the century, a smelter of large proportions was built and operated at Ranlett. It could not have been in operation much more than fifteen years as it was closed in the very early years of this century. Where records of its production might be unearthed is a question.

The depth of below-ground operations at any period were never in excess of four hundred feet; worked from two shafts and laterally encompassing probably no more than a half mile. Quite respectable, but minuscule in comparison with the 8,000 foot depth of shaft and 200 linear miles of drifts of the Argonaut, a typical big mine of the Mother Lode.

Two or three of the masonry structures of the smelter are still in position and are easily visible from highway 88.

Ranlett owned the largest of the road sheds. There were at least five on the old freight road to Jackson, now Highway 88. These spanned the road high overhead. In their length, they were adequate shelter for the ten-mule teams, allowing the tired animals to rest and cool off in the shade while they slaked their thirst at water troughs placed end to end at one side. These were in front of business establishments. On the opposite side, a saloon provided paralleling solace to the knights of the jerk line. Of these the greatest was Miller Station just west of Ranlett. It was a rambling, two-story, balconied wooden structure, enclosing an enormous barroom, restaurant, hotel facilities, and an outsize dance hall. In architecture it could be classified as cow country baroque. The outbuildings were a complex of stables, corrals, barns, granaries, and hay lofts.

The old Ranlett Post Office, a frame building of generous dimensions stood at the roadside until well into the nineteen-fifties. At its removal the post office sign, still in an excellent state of preservation, was taken to the museum at Jackson. It may be seen in the vehicle and transportation section.

We said that Ranlett had more lives than a cat. In World War II the demand for copper caused the old shafts to be opened and worked. At the end of the conflict it was closed again.

In the year 1965 a company took over the old workings and is presently engaged in the production of copper by methods, that if press accounts are to be credited, are practically identical with those described by Mason in 1881.

Copper Hill

The first notice that we have of Copper Hill appears in rather casual references in the *Sacramento Bee* to prospecting activities in search of the red metal south of the Cosumnes. Access to this part of the country was readily attained, in that the works and the inhabited portion lay astride of the original freightwagon road to the Southern Mines. This life line, in its several segments consisted of the river steamers connecting the wharves of San Francisco with the embarcadero at Sacramento. From thence the first rail line in California laid freight down in the warehouses at Folsom. From this base were two roads, one to the northern and one to the southern mines. The southern held a course several miles north of the Cosumnes and finally dropped down to river side and a crossing by means of the old Lamb Suspension Bridge. The stone work in the canyon on the lower side of the well-designed grade and the matching stone work on the bridge abutments and in the pylons that supported the cables attest to a high degree of engineering skill exhibited by the builders.

The old cables hung for many years and may well yet hang; draped across the stream a hundred feet above water. They are composed of a bundle of fibrous wrought iron wires spaghetti in size, four inches in diameter, entirely straight; the purity of the iron rendering them practically impervious to rust or corrosion. One wonders why this very fine road was abandoned in the late sixties in favor of a quite inferior line further to south. Explanation may turn out to be that, with the development of the Central Pacific track system in the direction of the Sierra crossing, the Folsom line was abandoned for the reason that the northern mines were served directly. The southern mines were forced to open a new route. In the period around and before the First World War there still remained, close to the north end of the bridge, a series of sheds and barns that housed freight and log wagons. There were Concord coaches, Hendersons, (sometimes called Buffalo Bill wagons), spring wagons, phaetons, landaus, surreys, buckboards, buggies, sulky carts; to mention a few. One suspects that a good part of the rolling stock of this '49 Appian Way came to journey's end right there. What would the museums and transportation exhibits offer for that which was casually allowed to rot down?

These sheds also contained equipment for use of the mine. The equipment; mine cars, (three different sizes), donkey engines, skips (several sizes down to winz buckets), track pipe, mostly wooden, to survive the action of the copper, conduit, cable, valves; all of the multiple items of hardware indispensable to the operation of a big mine. What became of all of this I do not know. But salvage at any reasonable price could have been more lucrative than mining.

The period from 1904 to the close of World War I was, if one is permitted to scramble a metaphor, the golden age of Copper Hill. The two shafts tapped the main ore body at a depth of three to four hundred feet. A line of ore wagons hauled the output past Forest Home to a rail siding near Clay Station. The old bridge was very lightly used and then its floor was ripped up leaving only a plank for foot traffic. As a thing of economics one wonders why the old bridge could not have been beefed up to a point where it could have served to make a hook-up with the rail siding at Latrobe: a distance of five miles north as against twenty miles south. A ton mile in the old days of wagon, mule, and rutted road was a very expensive item in terms of what we know. Whatever the reason it was not done.

Miners who worked at Copper Hill tell of an odd phenomenon. At around the Summer solstice the sun for some few days in the afternoon would line up on one of the incline shafts in such a way that its rays would go clear to the bottom. To a miner who had not been forewarned seeing this was a terrifying experience. Of all the myriad catastrophes that can strike below ground fire is the worst. For a few minutes of a few days in June Old Sol staged a visual imitation of the ultimate tragedy.

The close of the First World War broke the price of copper from thirty-five cents per pound to seven or less. Very few mines in the United States survived the impact. Copper Hill closed down.

In the Second World War a new shaft was sunk a half mile to the north. Limited production was terminated when war's end reduced the demand for copper.

We have perhaps gone lightly on a description of the town itself. The best edifice was the Gilbert house at the south end of the bridge. It seems to have antedated the others by years. The planting around it was beautiful and in good taste. Up the hillsides and out to the undulating area surrounding the shafts, the houses of the superintendent, underground foreman, and of the skilled workers sprawled in no recognizable order. Boarding houses and miner's cabins were just simply scattered around. In the entire span of its existence, Copper Hill never crystalized or jelled a business district, though at times several hundred people were present.

In the interval between wars, the gallows frames of the deserted mine reared their gaunt skeletons into the skyline. These were formed of timbers eighteen inches square, painted freight car red, and, for wooden structures, soared aloft to a seemingly alarming height.

Children and those who were no longer children achieved great thrills by climbing the stairs and ladders to the various platforms, peering into the ore bins, and, on a dare, making the final ascent to the railed flat surrounding the giant bull wheels.

Timbers, rotting at one side, overturned one of them. A grass and brush fire a few years later reduced both to a massed remnant of blackened and twisted metal.

In the interim a somewhat surprising return was harvested. The gouge dumps were covered with peacock rock, azurites and malachites of an iridescence and beauty not exceeded, one would suppose, in identical mineral anywhere on earth. The international brotherhood of rockhounds discovered the place, almost blew a fuse, and made a run on it. The owners, alerted to the situation, ejected the lapidarians and, in some arrangement with commercial interests dealing in that commodity, reaped what was by common report a handsome return.

One wonders why it apparently never occurred to the owners to open the mine just for the production of gem material. It may be of course that the particular formation producing the brilliant colors has been exhausted. It is doubtful if some of the recovered specimens have any counterpart anywhere. Some are of alternate thin slices of rainbow malachite and crystalline gold-bearing quartz, in the form of a sort of silicious Dagwood sandwich.

Musicdale

In telling the story of Musicdale we are not going to get much assistance from history or from any press clippings of the time. It survives in the remembrances of old timers who lived until after the turn of the century. By their accounts the earliest miners were Missourians, mostly from Pike County. Their fiddles were intact after the bone-breaking journey acros the continent and were employed in contests with the virtuosos of Fiddletown. Nothing documentary, but considering the name applied, this statement is at least coherent. We draw upon folklore for the assertion that several hundred miners worked at the sluice boxes in the inverted W bend of the river. The high slopes of the mountains confined their operations to the narrow bars which, by accounts that have come down to us, were quite rich.

Two old roads, still traceable, lead to the spot from the Amador side. One, much more shadowy at this time, snaked up a canyon on the El Dorado side. A pack trail, still in places recognizable as such, twined down the river on the southern bank from Nashville. This was probably the original link with the outside world.

Two ravines, draining to the river from the Amador side, held between them, at river's edge, a bench or low mesa. After a few hundred yards the ground rose rapidly as one made southing. Here were, and mayhap still are, old foundations, stone cellars and outlines of buildings. Until before the First World War several structures inhabitable by humans were in existence.

A style of architecture that might by fancy be termed Musicdalean—of which there still remained several specimens—was a tight board-and-batten thing of two rooms footed upon a cellar or basement built of stratified serpentine mortared with mud. The walls came about three feet above grade and were sunken to provide about seven feet of headroom under the floor. A compact functional dwelling with ample storage below.

One of these was occupied in pre-1914 days by an elderly, suave, and courteous gentleman called by his neighbors Mr. Lafferty. The nearest neighbors were seven miles distant. This is a bit curious in that I have seen him write his name. It came out like this, "Labarde." He owned with pride to being a native of La Belle France, and, with complete right, to being alcalde or mayor, as he was the last inhabitant. What little I know of Musicdale came from him. In youth one does not ask the questions that later seem to be so important.

Not by their initiative but by direct invitation of Mr. Labarde two 12 year-olds excavated in the basement of a collapsed and ruined structure. When whole it must have been an almost exact duplicate of the one occupied by our friend. I was one of those two.

A partial inventory of recovered treasures will list these as remembered best:

A .44 rimfire Henry rifle (no ammo), miraculously unrusted or corroded.

A berry set of bronze and green hobnail glass, unchipped or flawed.

Large bowl and eight matching dishes.

A box of perhaps 24 books, undamaged, dates of 1812 to 1822, by a Philadelphia publishing house, Subject matter: poems of Dryden, Pope, Southey, etc. Histories. Translations of the philosophical works of Voltaire, Rousseau, Diderot and much more, now forgotten.

A green glass bottle, almost globular of perhaps two quarts capacity. Possessed for many years until given to a bottle collector friend, in 1964. It created a small stir when exhibited in bottle collecting circles in the lower East Bay. By them it was identified as Chinese and very old.

Butte City

The one outstanding and remaining feature of the Butte City landscape is the Butte City Store desecrated by hoodlums and currently used as a quarry by vandals, whose acts are rapidly reducing it to an unrecognizable mound of stone. It has the misfortune to be right at the edge of Highway 49 and thus subject to the tender mercy of Swinus Americanus.

This store was erected in 1856 by E. Bruno Gionocchio and one Carrato, given name not of record. Mr. Gionocchio arrived at Butte City from Mariposa. At the time of its erection, Butte City was a town of six hundred houses. If standard formulas of five persons per unit are valid this postulates a population of three thousand.

The old records are in agreement in stating that it was a supply source of fruits and vegetables for a wide surrounding area. (Mason remarks upon the proliferation of orange trees and that the town appeared to be situated in a thermal.) Bouganvillea thrived on ramadas and even poinsettias were known to flourish when espaliered on a south-facing wall, which protected it from the north wind. This condition still obtains in its sister community of Mokelumne Hill on a corresponding table of the same elevation south of the river. Mokelumne Hill exhibits orange trees of giant size. Whatever the reason, the winter oranges (Washington Navels) adapt to the locale better than the Summer varieties, Valencias and such though even these produce adequately.

In mining, great riches were removed from partially impacted gravel formations at depths of from fifty to two hundred feet. The whole area north and northeast of the store is a booby trap of old shafts and ventilating outlets. The recovered gold was classified as alluvial. The methods of its recovery approximated those of the deep hardrock techniques though the Cousin Jacks with considerable scorn referred to all such operations as grass roots cleaning or robbing the gophers.

Excess water was a persistent impediment until a partial solution was effected by driving drainage tunnels a distance of miles out to the Mokelumne. An area of several square miles resembles nothing so much as a billet of timber that has been thoroughly worked out by termites or teredos.

Butte City and Mokelumne Hill were inhabited in the fifties by a people almost entirely Gallic. French was the language of the market place, the diggings, the public gathering, and the newspapers. Under the lash of assault from the criminal element attacking foreign groups, the French organized, armed, uniformed, and drilled militia companies for their protection. A fort was built and garrisoned above Mokelumne Hill. Here we have the logical Latin mind at work in a situation that their Anglo Saxon counterparts would have done well to copy. When their organization reached a certain level of competence they were severely let alone by the criminals. One cannot help but wonder if some of the older drill masters remembered the slope of Mont St. Jean, the hidden trap of the Hougomont Road, or the bayonet work around the farmhouse of La Haye Sainte. How many of them may we suppose, pulled G I time under the eagles of the Old Guard?

The end result was law and order and their possession

of the right to go about their business unmolested. There are some analogies between criminal pressure and electrical pressure. Both divide inversely to the square of the resistance.

The record of the French in California is both high and honorable. They were held in affectionate regard by their decent English speaking fellow miners. They acquired the appelation Kes-kee-dees, (ca est ca dit?) What are they saying?—a common expression of the French when hearing their American neighbors in conversation. Many of their descendants live in the Mother Lode and are numbered among its most substantial citizens.

Hardly a trace of the old orchards, vineyards, and plantings remain. A once thriving community is a scene of desolation.

Doschville

The first use of the great clay resources around Ione occurred in 1854. In the previous years the discovery was probably made incidental to the frantic quest for the yellow metal. The first pit was opened to commercial use close to the present position of the Indian Hill Plant of Gladding McBean or Interpace. The town of Doschville grew within a stone's throw of these works. We draw upon local tradition for the statement that one Mr. Dosch was the individual responsible for this first successful venture in the exploitation of the County's resources of usable alumina. Very little or nothing seems to be extant upon his life or background. Perhaps the archives of the State Bureau of Mines if thoroughly researched would yield something.

Several of the Doschville business buildings, quite

typically Mother Lode in pattern, stone with iron doors and shutters formerly lined the south side of the Michigan Bar Road directly opposite the Indian Hill Plant. Like the ten little Indians on the gate they went down one by one until there remained a lone survivor up until around 1950. This was scraped out for no apparent reason other than that someone wanted to see if the blade on the D 8 was performing as it should. It was. And now, of Doschville, we have nothing.

West of the highway, just north of the railway road crossing to the plant under a grove of great oaks there are four shallow depressions in the earth of exactly gravelike outline and dimensions.

These, by legend, are the last resting places of four horsethieves, seized and hung by a posse sometime in the 1860's. The story goes that they were given the choice of a flogging or the noose. To their eternal credit in their final moment of truth they stood tall and died like men. This tale has no way of either being substantiated or refuted but it may well have happened.

Irishtown

The marker below Pine Grove stands on the south side of Highway 88. The town may well have crossed the road but most remnants of it are on the North. It appears to have been removed a sufficient distance from Pine Grove to have preserved its separate identity. The environs are loaded with a maze of old stone walls, building bases, fragments of old orchards and vineyards. In spring, apple, pear, and plum in bloom cast their fragrance down wind.

Past the century's turn two old wells powered, or

rather, served, by long sweeps, were bait for artists. What wielder of the brush can resist getting out palette, tubes, camel's hair, and spatula at sight of the old pendent bucket, perfect as were those of iron hooped oak, long spruce beam, and counterweighting box of boulders.

There seems to be no tenable explanation as to why communities adjacent to each other and with almost identical sources of building material frequently elected to go down entirely different paths. National origins of the builders in this case give us no clue to the riddle at all. Pine Grove was, and mostly is, a town of wood with a few burned brick units at intervals. Irishtown was at least at center entirely adobe. These massive walls stood until thirty or forty years ago, open to the sky, the windows sightless quadrangles, the snow rain and frost year on year prying the cream colored plaster from its red-brown base, the iron doors pulling from their hinges and lying in rusting abandonment across the entrances. Massive lintels of oak, moss covered, weathered to a dull green, grass growing on top, and host to those wild flowers whose seeds are windborn.

In the building of these, a technique was used of surprising effectiveness, which seemed to have been not too common. Instead of chopped straw, pine needles were used in the brick-making as a binder. It yielded a product whose strength appears to have been at least equal or superior to the conventional product. Buildings so constructed were extremely durable. Over in Calaveras, a block of business buildings in West Point so produced, testifies to its permanence in that they are in use to this day. Mountain Ranch, further south, owns several of great size; one being of two stories, that are all serving their owners well.

We close our brief account of Irishtown with a touch of nostaglia and a bit of sadness. The writer of these lines first saw the light of day very close hereby.

Where the Sons of Erin went there went the violins.

Rammed earth structure at the head of Spanish Gulch.

Houses of this type, over a hundred years old, are still in use.

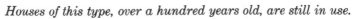

A Horno, or bake oven, believed to be an invention of the American Indian.

Fallen Chimney and foundation stones at French Camp.

This is Buttonwillow's famous Buttonwillow tree.

Smokestack at the ruined gold smelter at Rancheria.

Full length view of the same stack. It was built in 1854.

North abutment and approach—Morrow's bridge over the Mokelumne.

Rocker grid, bedplate, and shovel, photographed as found at Quien Sabe.

These walls, now returned to their parent earth, once echoed the strains of Johnny Flynn, The Mooncoyn Reel, and Tipperary in the Morning.

Irish Hill

Geologists inform us that the Irish Hill gravels are a mixture of the marine formation found at Muletown and the type encountered in the streams formed since the block of the Sierra Nevada tilted to the West.

The townsite is an irregular acreage of cobbled mounds. Buildings are non-existent. The oft-repeated pattern of a town destroyed when riches were discovered beneath it. The usual set-up of sluices operated at the arrival of a ditch, in this case the Plymouth Ditch bringing water from the Cosumnes. With water available at high pressures the change wrought in the scenery is exceeded nowhere in Amador and has few doubles anywhere in the Lode.

The long hogback behind the town was attacked with the monitors, cut clear around, and turned into a colossal, red-sided, green-topped Noah's Ark. The red of the sides; the iron oxide loaded clay, the top; a cover of dense chemise.

Hydraulic mining at Irish Hill continued to a much later date than at the neighboring diggings. This was made practicable by dams built below the scene of operations which impounded the slickens and therefore drew no fire from the anti-silt regulations.

Several small houses or rather semi-cabins remained near the original town site until a relatively recent date. These were occupied by the crews engaged in the final clean-up of the giants.

At roadside an Irish saloon outlasted them all. This has a sound of being entirely too pat. But things have a way of being that way sometimes and so it was here. The proprietor was a friend of James Moore.

This was a welcome oasis to those engaged in a cow drive from Forest Home to Ione or vice versa and a port of call for all and sundry having business in those parts in that horse drawn era.

Every nationality had their own saloons each as distinct as the ethnic group that produced it, though the entire population patronized all of them with no resentment or discrimination whatsoever and entire friendliness all around.

This saloon was a thing of board and batten of fair dimensions fronted not by a road shed but what might be termed a sort of port-cochere. There were many Irish saloons in the Mother Lode. This was a fair example of one that might be termed in the middle range of affluence and decor, and so, fairly typical. Let us go inside and take a look.

Quarter round shields at the two outer corners of the polished walnut bar; one proclaiming the virtues of Guiness Stout, the other of Dublin Stout. Enameled medallions above the respective racks of the product of John Jamieson and Son and Jamieson Ltd., testifying to their excellence.

The pictures on the walls: Photos of John L. Sullivan and Paddy Ryan in ring stance, bare knuckled, in black tights and spiked shoes. Many pictures of race horses. There may have been an old-time Irishman who was not a passionate lover of horses and an avid follower of the Sport of Kings. If there was such, I never met him. In the race horse pictures the place of honor in the center was given to the greatest of the great of all in harness racing, the nonpareil, the incomparable "Dan Patch."

On the opposite wall under glass on green silk a thing of elfin beauty from dainty feminine hands: The Harp of

Tara embroidered in scarlet and gold thread. The companion piece:—A painting that must have plucked at many a heart string—the last look that many generations of Irish outward bound from Cork ever had of their homeland: The ruined castle at the Head of Old Kinsale.

Upper Rancheria

In the years following the time of trouble, the whole area—abandoned by living humans and repossessed by the forces of nature—was left to itself. I was told, when a small boy, by my father, that by common consent both groups had no desire to re-occupy the blood-stained ground.

Cowmen in the small years of this century in search of stray steers reported riding into and down a long street lined by great stone buildings, some of them of, two, and one, of three, stories, their burnt out shells throwing their skeleton forms against the skyline. To this day that entire country is completely uninhabited.

An examination of the townsite will show that it was built around the foot of an almost perfectly circular mountain, flat at the top, the buildings forming half of the hub of a wheel.

This scene of ruin and desolation, discovered by artists perhaps thirty years ago was the source of canvases of great beauty that were exhibited on the West Coast and perhaps were viewed in an even wider circle.

If one wishes to bring utter destruction, desecration, and befoulment upon a ghost town, all that is necessary is to let its site be widely known. And by an inverse reaction these paintings accomplished just that.

One by one, using the advanced techniques of modern

engineering these structures were numbered, part by part, disassembled, transported, and re-erected at points far and wide in exactly the same way that William Randolph Hearst caused monasteries and churches in Spain and Italy to be moved to San Simeon.

The very last remaining building, the Stone Jug was removed and re-erected in Volcano in the 1950's. At the site, if one does not take into account cellars and basements, not one stone remains atop another.

At nightfall, if a word from the present inhabitants is desired, one must listen to the wail of the coyote from the thickets of madrone and the whoo-whoo-whoo of the moping owl on the bluff overhead.

American Flat

In the press notices of the time and the comment upon the anarchy, riot, and bloodshed rampant in the area of the Rancherias—of which, incidentally, American Flat is at the point of a triangle formed by the two Rancherias at the base—much material is given to the formation of posses and armed citizens' groups. And, also, one notes with sadness the rise of bands of hoodlums and vandals who were the main contributors to these happenings. Documentation, is here that this community on the Dead Man's Fork was in this terrible business right up to its neck.

In the whole area of these three towns, one does not need to be psychic or oversensitive to experience a feeling of depression and a desire to terminate the visit as soon as possible. This was observed by several members of the party of the U.S. Geological Survey who mapped the area in the early 1960's and had no previous knowledge of the dark history in the background.

The topography of the town shows that part of it was built upon a boat shaped bit of ground and that this was overflowed. The buildings pushed up the steep north slope. This portion is pretty well obliterated by the returning forest. Trees, their trunks thirty inches in diameter and growing close together, make any study or tracing of the walls and foundations a real obstacle course.

On the south side of the boat, the tall pines march in stately ranks up the mountain side. Through them, an ancient road that once resounded to the drumming hoofs of the mounts of Claudio, Three Fingered Jack, and Luis Guerra, turns, twists, and loops to a point at the summit that leads to nowhere.

Lower Rancheria

The old writers always speak of lower Rancheria as being on a steep incline or pitch of the main Mother Lode, which in this area they state achieves a gradient of forty-five per cent. This is head on with all published maps. They show the Lode, where it surfaces, as being miles west and running approximately through Amador City—to give this as being the nearest point to Rancheria.

An attempt at resolving these two opposed positions might run somehing like this: the early writers may have had in mind the East Lode. For more than a century, the assertion or denial of the existence of the East Lode is enough to launch a controversy among mining men that is far from being resolved at this date.

A factor that may assist in a partial compromise of these two stands is this: whether or no it does exist there is an outcropping separated in places by miles, of quartz that at some points is of great richness, that is roughly in paralleling alignment to the main Mother Lode. Upon this line are found the Defender, Climax, and Rainbow mines to mention but a few, that from pocket formations or veins that varied tremendously in content, did at times and in places pay handsomely. Of course the great and enormously productive mines of the Grass Valley-Nevada City complex as illustrated by the Empire, the Idaho Maryland, and the North Star are all on the East Lode.

Now let us try for a synthesis in that the difference appears to narrow to this; that the outcroppings are or are not connected by a magma at great depth. When and if this depth is sounded we will have the answer.

There are many references in the fifties, before the enactment of the tragedy, to arrastres and chile mills that were giving a high return. Arrastres powered by water get frequent mention. This is most unusual, and—astonishingly enough—one comes to notice, of which steam was the moving force. However, nothing of the record can be located that shows any effort was expended upon deep hard rock mining.

Deep Gulch and Slate Gulch were tremendously rich and were said to equal or surpass anything in the county, the area of Lancha Plana being excepted.

Now, as we must, we come to the terrible thing that must be told. Of a gang of twelve Mexicans that were first reported at Jacalitos and traced to Drytown where a show of force drove them off. Descending upon Rancheria they murdered eight persons on Aug. 6, 1855.

A posse gathered by Phoenix, the first sheriff of Amador tracked them on a twisted trail that ended in a gun battle at a big adobe cantina and casa de baile on the west face of Bear Mountain in Calaveras on Aug.

12, 1855. The gallant sheriff was killed as were also several members of the posse and several of the posse were wounded. An undetermined number of the bandits were killed, the rest escaping to the brush behind the building.

This next is even worse. The disarming, murder, indignities, violence, and expulsion visited upon the whole peaceful Mexican population of the Rancherias, Drytown, and adjacent areas, culminating in the burning of the Catholic Church of Drytown. This outrage brought out the decent elements of the communities in an at least partially successful restoration of law and order.

All of this is here sketched as briefly as possible. The whole account is given in detail by Mason, to which anyone interested is referred.

These gruesome happenings are thought to have been an aftermath of the killing of Joaquin Murrieta, Three Fingered Jack, and several of the band at the Arroyo Cantova by the California Rangers, captained by Harry Love on July 23, 1853. Out of all of this came the abandonment of the entire country round about, by both Americans and Mexicans. This is fully documented in County archives that list several hundred registered voters resident in the early 1850's and not a solitary one as of 1860.

Old stone footings of massive buildings sprawl across the base of Quartz Mountain and out onto the flat, any order or sequence that they may originally have possessed being obscured by returning vegetation. At roadside a granite marker of generous dimensions centers a long concrete slab covering the graves of several members of the Dynan family including Mary, who was one of those killed by the bandits on Aug. 6, 1855. This very beautiful work of remembrance was erected by a grandson of R. H. Dynan in 1941.

At a distance of perhaps 100 yards southwest, in the center of a grassy meadow, a fence protects a small cemetery shaded by a lone oak of colossal size. Here are grouped the marble tablets bearing the epitaphs of other victims of the massacre, together with other internments, nearly all within the date bracket of the decade 1850 to 1860.

Summit City

What we have here in terms of geography and minerology fits more into the frame or context of Nevada than that of California. What happened at Summit City, or whatever forces brought it into being, appears to be the result or an end product of the exploration for silver; undertaken first at Silver City in Alpine County and extended South-East to the Amador Line. This community, of which, be it said, that it is almost impossible to locate any actual history, was probably the far end of a wave at its extremity, a mere ripple of the exploratory forces, tidal in their intensity, that were generated by the discovery of the literal silver mountains of the Comstock.

The various tunnels and inclines do not yield any clue to the writer as to how well they had done in their prospect, for the reason that, unfortunately, he is not at all versed in the mineralogy of silver. The conditions under which mining was accomplished were so difficult as to be beyond belief. From early November or sometimes into July the High Sierra is in the grip of King Winter. Snow in depths of eight to thirty-five feet seals all roads and trails. Skis and snow shoes are useless against cliffs, crevasses, and slot gorges. With all of the resources of science and engineering at the disposal of the road maintenance crews, the transcontinental highways and railways are sometimes closed for days and even weeks. In the nineteen fifties two hundred passengers were spared their lives by a tiny margin when the California-bound train stalled at the face of a forty-foot snow drift at Norden. Weeks of concerted effort by all of the resources of a great state finally achieved succor. Relief came in on the backs of expert ski men, trained and hardened in the techniques of arctic exploration and survival. Snow plows and helicopters were utterly useless in the face of the roar of the blizzard. It is by no means impossible that at some future date a reenactment of the tragedy at Donner Lake may take place. Not a season passes but that lives are lost when someone leaves the main highway and is caught by a storm down in a side canyon. In below zero cold, with no reserves of food or clothing, death comes quickly. In Winter do not dare the storm Gods of the Sierra unless you feel that you must.

This high country, when Mid-Summer rolls back the snow in the passes, is as barren as the craters of the moon. Far below, in sheltered niches and folds in the rock, twisted tamarack and stunted silvery quakenash fight for life and a tiny bit of growth in the short ninety days granted to them. Melting snow banks generate pools of water that nourish skunk cabbage into thickets that spring up at mushroom speed. The wax red of the snow flowers renew their endless cycle as the snow retreats and they follow.

In one of these small lakes, there stood for many decades, at its upper end, three old prairie schooners partially submerged, decaying down to their skeletons of iron work. A story that can hardly be firmed up enough to be called a legend tells that they were abandoned during an Indian attack. If so this would appear to have been a repeat of the affair at Tragedy Springs.

Mile on mile may. be traced the tracks, worn inches deep in the granite of snow-polished domes and ridges by the narrow tires of black Norway iron of the seven foot wheels of the old conestigas. How many passed this way say you to have carved a record so deep?

In exploration of this upper world on the old immigrant road one is impressed by the number of graves encountered. Graves are scattered everywhere that a scanty bit of soil might be excavated in a rock crevice and a cairn of stone built from the talus mass at the base of the granite peaks. Here is evidence that, after two thousand miles of hardship and suffering, at the last barricade before the promised land in all too many cases, tired spirits and bodies were broken in the scaling of the mighty rampart of the Sierra Nevada.

Into Summit City a pack train could penetrate in July, August, and September. A thousand feet above the town a branch of the old road ends just like that. Heavier freight was lowered into one of the greatest canyons on earth by means of blocks and tackles belayed to iron axles driven into holes single-jacked into the living rock by daring young men on flying bosun's chairs.

This was a repeat of the method used at the Carson Spur where some of the old iron bars are still in view, to which the falls were attached to haul up the wagons that were dis-assembled to make this possible. The oxen were taken up in belly bands and all re-assembled at the summit.

The builders of Summit City were of the breed of Paul Bunyan.

In the ruins of the town a few stone walls and house foundations may have lasted to this day. An artifact of more than passing interest was the remnant of a pool table. The mechanics of lowering such an object over a sheer precipice of that height are of course impossible. But it was done because there it is. For a moment let us consider the motivation behind this. Eight months of total confinement and complete isolation in that white hell is more than the spirit of man may endure, more especially when it is inflicted upon a small group. Under such conditions cabin fever is a more deadly menace than a bullet. For this poison, the pool table was at least a partial antidote. May we express our unbounded admiration for the townsmen of Summit City; of all of the rugged and durable, the most rugged and durable.

Forest Home

In the flow, interplay, contacts, groupings, polarizations, and stratifications of all nationalities, economic levels, culture, learning, and degrees of competence, occasionally there is encountered a group crystalizing from a single geographical origin. We may well use Forest Home as an example of this, where if not a majority, at least a wide segment of the inhabitants hailed from the Wolverine State. This held true to clear across the line into the County of Sacramento where Michigan Bar by its name proclaimed the native state of most of its citizens.

The cemetery on the hill north-east of town documents this quite well; its epitaphs giving Michigan as the state of origin of many of those laid to rest. This necropolis holds some impressive headstones, several large shortened obelisks of marble and two massive, above grade, tombs formed of slabs of marble weighing tons, encircled by a fence of lacy black iron. One headstone bears the regimental crest of a veteran of the War of 1812.

One of the most beautiful and stately stone structures within the entire county is now a shapeless mound atop the hill west of the town center and facing Highway 16 at its south side. Reduced to a shell by wave upon wave of vandals, its 24-inch thick walls of buff colored cut stone were purposely collapsed to prevent injury or possibly death to some thoughtless sightseer. In the mold so often repeated, a giant Washington palm and several spiked agaves bear witness to the once extensive landscaping in the grounds adjacent.

Several miles up the Cosumnes a diversion dam turned water into a ditch serving the placers. This ditch is probably the largest in the Mother Lode. It is perhaps twelve feet wide at the bottom and six feet deep, flaring to twenty feet of width at the top. The area that it served was of many miles square. With the possible exception of Dutch Flat and Blue Canyon this rerouting of a river on this scale was attempted nowhere else.

The underlying formation here is a saffron-pink quartz gravel. Records of its content of precious metal do not seem to be locatable at least not in any county files. These gravels, when taken from well washed deposits in the creek bottoms and used as aggregate in concrete making, yield a product that possesses great strength.

Fort John

In natural beauty there is not one of these sites that equals Fort John. A little meadow at the bottom of a slot canyon is bounded on one side by the babbling headwaters of Amador Creek. Enough of the virgin forest, supported by dense second growth, clothes the canyon walls at north and south with a veritable fairyland, the light, filtering down through the greenness a hundred and fifty feet overhead, inspires reverence when one penetrates to these sylvan depths of a great cathedral of nature.

On the meadow, wild rose, columbine, and a dozen other of the wild flowers of the Sierra bloom and proliferate in wild abandon. Remnants of old orchards set their blossoms in spring, in cadence with their wild relatives. One old almond tree has attained a diameter of three feet at its base and is still growing. Its fruit, no doubt, has long since reverted to the wild and turned bitter, as almonds always do when not tended and cultivated.

Access to the site from the east is effected by a road that hugs the north wall of the canyon. A mile or so of its lower reach was formed by blasting the granite out of the sheer face of the mountain, building a retaining wall at the lower side from the fragmented stone, this wall, in its entire length, being from five to fifty feet in height, and finally filling in the space between the cliff and the wall with earth. The labor and explosives that went into this is a thing to contemplate and bears witness to the one-time importance of the place.

There is no evidence upon the crowned surface of the roadbed that an iron tire of a horse drawn vehicle or the rubber tread of automotive equipment has turned here in the last seevnty-five or perhaps one hundred years.

There is a maze of filled-in cellars, wall footings, foundation outlines, and one structure that, in this whole series, has no counterpart. This is a thing of fieldstone mortared in adobe and inletted into the grade at the north. There is a discernible wall above it and, up the slope, there is the base of a much larger building, of which this structure served as a lower story. In its present ruined state one can note that it carried a topping of massive timbers, covered by at least two feet of earth. Fire slits are placed in the wall in such a manner that a complete sweep of the area adjacent is obtained by intersecting lines of aim. Observing the embrasured openings in their rear or interior faces, it would appear, and this is only an estimate, no protractor or azimuth being at hand, that the traverse or arc of small arms fire would be about sixty degrees.

A trapdoor through the earth deck would enable men

to assemble for a last ditch stand, safe from fire, and able to mount a murderous counteroffensive from the loopholes. The larger building above it probably functioned as arsenal, magazine, guard room, and of course the point of final resistance.

On the physical evidence this must have been a much more important post than Fort Ann. No information can be located apparently as to how many men were stationed here, how long they remained, or when the site lost its military significance.

When we turn from field exploration to documentary, we encounter an odd twist: The statement that, in 1850, by one account, twenty-nine miners assembled and formed the first temperance society in California. This organization grew and grew, and, if we are to credit their press releases, doubtless overly optimistic, they really had the Demon Rum on the ropes.

A disproportionately large amount of news items originating thereabouts in the 1850's and early 60's is given to the expansion of the Temperance Peoples' activities. The claim of a membership of from five to six hundred persons in the Society is made as early as 1854.

At the mid 1860's as good a point as any to close this brief account mention is made of an approximate one thousand people who gathered at the town hall to pay their disrespects to John Barleycorn.

Misery Flat

In an era in which the written and spoken word is entirely dominated by semantics it is refreshing to contemplate a time when things were called by their right names. In the history of California both the Spanish and the English tongues were forthright and precise in their nomenclature. Casa Mala, Los Muertos, La Canada del Hambre, and El Rio de las Putas scored right in the ten ring. In Old Saxon, Blood Gulch, Tragedy Springs, Dead Man's Fork, and Misery Flat were likewise bullseyes.

John Doble with his acute sensitivity and compassion notes the wretched condition of the immigrants as they drew nigh to Volcano. East of the town at Misery Flat, clover-laden meadows and abundant fresh water contributed healing balm and comfort to worn out man and beast after their fearsome ordeal.

It is doubtful if any structures more elaborate than a few rude board-and-batten cabins or log enclosures were ever erected, but hundreds of people occupied the environs, the most transient of populations: so, under our ground rules, it qualifies as a town even though it may compete with Jacalitos for the title of most ephemeral.

An exception to the above statement of the light character of the buildings was a layout used for the shoeing of oxen that lasted until well into the twentieth century. As is the case of so much of that with which we are dealing, there was, not so long ago, so much of it around and then, seemingly all at once, it was all gone.

This was the device: an enormous wooden wheel, twenty or more feet in diameter spoked into a foot thick log windlass drum, the outer perimeter of the wheel carrying in a groove, a rope. This afforded a tremendous leverage against the hoisting tackle rove around the drum. With a sling placed under the animal's mid-section one man could hoist a beast of a half ton weight or more, with ease. One detail that is missing from this assemblage, and did not survive the passage of time, was whatever method was used to prevent the ox from kicking the farrier into the adjoining county.

The last of the ox-shoeing establishments, of which the writer has any knowledge, stood an approximate half-mile north of Myers Station on Highway 50 until the nineteen twenties.

If its site could be rediscovered a mine detector would turn out small half moon shaped iron plates and tiny nails exactly in the form of horse shoe nails but no more than three quarters of an inch in length.

Here we are contemplating an art, a technique, a subculture, call it what you will, that is completely gone. The bull men, a breed as specialized as the teamsters, the cowboys, or the mountain men are these many years extinct. This is why movies and TV show horse drawn equipment. There are now no oxen or drivers, though they supplied the power for the great wave that swept over the West.

Into the twentieth century the logging at Whitmore's saw mill used oxen in getting in the logs. There was no evidence of a hoist thereabouts. Quite probably they were shod at Misery Flat.

At the Days of '49 celebration at Sacramento in August of 1922, ox teams and covered wagons from the Mother Lode passed in their final review.

Enterprise

This community had its beginning at approximately the same time as Plymouth and Pokerville. Big Indian Creek held placer gold in amounts that drew the miners from the neighboring diggings to the number of hundreds. Outcroppings of seams from the Mother Lode, which this creek very closely parallels in its final northerly course to the Cosumnes, caused an early shift from placer to hardrock explorations. The results obtained varied from quite good to indifferent. Here we draw upon tradition and scanty and incomplete records.

This we do know. From these operations there developed three mines in the lode quartz of considerable size: The Enterprise, The Bay State, and the Ballard. There does not seem to be any source where one might get any information upon their total production. They appear to have expanded to their maximum output sometime in the 1890's. The Bay State was active until well past the turn of the century. Taking the evidence of their surface activities and what physically remains of these, one would place them in the order of their importance thus: The Bay State, the Enterprise, and the Ballard.

Drawing now upon Mother Lode lore: the reason for the abandonment of the operations was that water in overwhelming quantity was encountered beyond the capacity of any pumps then existent to clear, and in a maddening pattern that fate so often forms, this happened at precisely the point where rich ore was discovered in abundance.

Chinese, in the standard way of the placers, worked out that which had been missed by the earlier waves of miners. Their cabins lined both sides of the creek for several miles. A few resisted the assault of time and the elements until forty years ago. As mentioned in the bit on Lancha Plana, there is not a more tricky subject than an estimate of the number of Chinese in a given locality in the olden time; two hundred perhaps, five hundred possibly.

In the late twenties and early thirties small gold dredges called doodlebugs scraped out the bottom of Big Indian Creek and reaped a handsome return.

In the returning forest along the creek, pleasant summer homes have been established by persons seeking a vacation and week-end respite from the perils and tensions of the asphalt jungle. Along the watercourse itself, the beaver, no longer subject to the merciless pressure of the trappers, fell the ash, beech, and birch trees and construct beautiful dams.

Spanish Gulch

From its confluence with Dry Creek, Spanish Gulch extends due north for a mile and a half. It is lined with crumbling chimneys and building foundations—the many times repeated lay-out of the string bean town that sprang up along a water course.

A ruined building of quarried and cut stone coursed in lime mortar stands on a little hummock at the junction of the gulch with Dry Creek. Its outer wall has a fireplace of which the back measures twelve feet in width. This is quite the largest that has been encountered at any of the sites. This structure, on the evidence that it presents, must have served some public or semi-public need. What that was has small chance of ever being known.

As has been said before some communities, of which hardly a physical vestige survives, bulk large in the news and comment of the early days. Conversely, extensive construction in the best of durable materials go unnoticed in the early press, and in some cases even a name is hard, or sometimes impossible, to discover. Of these two categories Spanish Gulch groups in the latter. We do have the name and that is just about all.

At the upper end of the gulch a *tapia* or rammed earth house, still, as of this writing, standing gives point to what was said of the durability of this type of construction in the prologue. Within less than a hundred yards of this, a cemetery still owns a protecting fence and marking headstones. The epitaphs are mostly indecipherable due to the weathering of more than a century. Upon a very few the dates that are legible are those of the 1850's.

North of this cemetery a distance of perhaps fifty yards three arrastres are still recognizable. An explanation of this statement is probably in order. In the depression years, most of them were broken up and destroyed by the great army of snipers that invaded the old diggings, scratching for meagre returns that even the Chinese, preceding them by two or three generations, would have scorned. The beds and even the guide walls of the arrastres were taken apart and the stones washed to glean the pitiful remnant of precious metal. For this reason an unwrecked specimen is a rarity, though they do exist.

One of these three mentioned above is quite unusual, in that the king post or pivoting bar, and the sweep, are of heavy iron. One could go far afield indeed to duplicate this.

Aqueduct

When nature applies herself to creating a park, in all of the world she has never exceeded herself in those mountain meadows at levels of from three to five thousand feet on the west slope of the Sierra Nevada. At the departure of the Winter snows, a ground nourished rainbow explodes across the little valleys with Indian clover, tiger lily, mariposa lily, iris, and that most breath-taking of all the wild flowers of the Sierra, the pendant spiked lanterns of the pink columbine. In the watercourses, crimson azaleas in masses load the breeze with perfume for miles downwind. This is curious and the botanists might offer an explanation as to why the domesticated relations of the azalea are so completely inert and unfragrant in complete contrast to their sylvan sisters.

The effect of all of this upon the immigrants was given to me in vivid imagery by my friend Bill Hoss, now these more than fifty years at peace. He told of the incredulous joy of the members of the train of which his folks were a part, and he a small boy, as they unyoked their worn out oxen and turned them loose to graze in the masses of clover and their people went to bathe in the icy waters of the little streams. Small effort on the part of those ambulant brought in hazel nuts from the ravines, wild raspberries and yew berries, and, by the hatful, the most incredibly delicious of all fruits, wild strawberries. No doctor could have prescribed a diet more healthful and calculated to offset the ravages of scurvy and malnutrition. "At night," said he, "we drifted to slumber to the sound of water rattling over the stones. This, after hundreds of miles of desert, and we were lulled to rest by that most soothing and inspiring of all music under Heaven, the roar of the wind in the two hundred foot tall cathedral of the sugar pines at the meadow's edge."

Such a paradise could not long remain unspoiled. In no time at all log and board-and-batten habitations mushroomed. Worm fences of rails split out of the giant cedars inclosed an adjacent acre or two, preserving that much grazing for the family cow and a horse or two.

Hard upon this came the next cycle. Gold in good paying quantities was discovered at the head waters of Sutter Creek. Assays of scattered outcroppings of the Blue Lead, that colossal dead river of the Pliocene time showed startling values. That did it. Overnight a town crowded out the little homesteads. A town containing, then or now, as it must, all of the headaches and dislocations that pop out of Pandora's box when humans elect, or are pressured, to dwell in close proximity to each other.

A great flume was constructed to bring the waters of Panther Creek, Tiger and Mill Creeks down to the placers. It crossed the little valley high overhead and most appropriately gave the place its name, "Aqueduct." This survived until well into the twentieth century. If there are any pictures of this existant and there must be some, somewhere, please believe them when they show its great height. At a guess one would say eighty feet. In the comings, goings, and doings of record in the press of the 1850's and 60's, yes and 1870's, Aqueduct takes its full share.

In the inevitable decline, a way station for the teams of the great log wagons outlasted all other structures. This was a long, two-storied balconied affair that catered mostly to the needs of the teamsters. Across the road a complex of barns, granaries, and sheds housed and provided for the animals. There were many such establishments in those days, now all of them have disappeared;

New York Ranch, Central House, Finn Ranch to mention a few. Not even a ghost of them around now.

The proprietor of this caravansery was Captain Glenn, a Civil War veteran. Of him a word or two might be said. He was wont to get together with Wallace Stewart of Pine Grove and perhaps a dozen or so of the other old G. A. R. men. Together they formed an orchestra or more accurately started a fife and drum corps. On national holidays Memorial Day, Fourth of July and such they would assemble their combo in full uniform. Is there anything more toe-tingling than the rattling slat of snare drums and the squeal of fifes in the hands of the skilled? They would beat out Haste to the Wedding, The Girl I left Behind Me, When Johnny Comes Marching Home, Captain Jenks of the Horse Marines.

To a small boy it made oh so vivid and real the stories that they told: Of the night that Atlanta burned, the whole firmament a wall of flame right up to zenith in the North-West, lighting the whole country to the brightness of a Mid-summer noon. Some of these oldsters had been in the Army of the Ohio of John McAllister Scofield, this being one of the three great armies under the command of William Tecumseh Sherman.

They told of the sergeants calling sidestep right or left, off of the road to let pass a battery of field artillery, the horses belly down at a run, the riders leaning flat from their saddles, the cannoneers clinging to the bolsters of the caissons for their very lives. Up ahead they would wheel out, unlimber, fire five or six salvos, this in the incredible time of three or four minutes out of muzzle loading pieces. Then, up limbers and away before the ranging shell of a Confederate battery found them and solved all of their earthly problems. They spoke with great respect of the Reb artillery and of the marksmanship of the gunners in butternut, fearsomely outnumbered and outweighed as they were. Out across the meadows, wheat fields, and orchards endless columns of blue clad infantry, moving south-east toward Savannah, sometimes raised their voices in the song: Kingdom Come or the Year of Jubilee. All of this must have been beyond the power of Dante to describe. A twice told tale. All of the original narrators are gone with the departure of Alfred Woolson in 1959 so whatever we have has to be second hand or out of the shelves of the library.

Of all of the G. A. R. men that I have known and of my acquaintance with the Old Rebs, hatred was no part of the make-up of any of them. Each held the other in affectionate respect for giving to the cause in which they believed, as Lincoln said so magnificently, "The last full measure of devotion."

At about the time of the First World War, improved roads and the advent of trucks retired the long jerk line teams. Aqueduct Station was torn down. Captain Glenn, Wallace Stewart, and their friends departed to the Elysian Fields. A place so charming could not long stay deserted. Summer homes and estates are now partially or wholly concealed in the surrounding forest. Up the road from the old townsite, neat and well kept orchards of apple and pear do much to retain for the place its oldtime appeal and beauty.

Jackass Gulch

As is the case with Jackass Hill over in Tuolumne, here we have a name that was applied at a very early date. The cargadores of the pack trains delighted in finding a meadow enclosed by impenetrable brush or surrounded by the walls of a box canyon and supplied with water by a live stream. Here the tired beasts could be unloaded and unsaddled and turned loose to pasture and recuperate for more labors when rested. This site fits the above description of the meadow, the water, and the encircling thicket of chemise perfectly.

Hardly any references to this place are extant in newspapers or publications of the time of its building. Counterbalancing this we encounter considerable evidence of a town of substance and importance.

The chimneys are, for the most part, still standing. Some of them are of carefully cut stone beautifully coursed and mortared. Several outsize basements or cellars, paved and walled up with the same materials used in the chimneys, evidence a community that endured for some considerable time. Some of these, at a guess, might have been wine cellars or even enclosures for brewery vats. Documentation for or against does not apparently exist.

It is known that a sawmill operated here for years. Hardly a stick of millable timber may now be found within a radius of ten miles.

Whatever was left was obliterated in a great fire in the Summer of 1906. This, starting at a point near Sunnybrook on what is now Highway 88 blackened thousands of acres, destroyed a number of ranch houses and outbuildings, roared up the canyon of Jackson Creek, and destroyed everything flammable at Jackass Gulch. What was left after the embers cooled was probably just about what is visible now.

At the lower edge of the town south of the creek a great cut was made in the canyon wall and faced with the high quality of stone work described previously. This appears to have been part of the structure containing the mill. The footings of the carriages, conveyors, steam engine, and other equipment essential to the operation can be made out without too much overuse of the imagination. It is most certain that after all wooden portions of the building burnt, all usable machinery was removed and the unusable metal was salvaged by the junk collectors.

Santa Maria Gulch

Not one of our ghost towns exceeds this one in complete isolation. There remains no trace of a wagon road. Access to this camp had to be by pack train and saddle horse; up the canyon of the Mokelumne, left hand into the throat gorge of Grapevine Gulch, then right handed into the draw of Santa Maria. A handful of riflemen could hold the approaches against a great number. Grapevine Gulch and the Mokelumne River bed are of course now deep beneath the waters of Lake Pardee. Fifteen or twenty old chimneys, several quadrangular welts that were evidently once adobes, an outline of a street, and that is it.

Documentation has not yet been discovered if any does exist. By methods somewhat analogous to that of a paleontologist, who can take a left front toe bone and reconstruct for us a complete bronthosaurus, let us take what remains at this obviously once well inhabited place and see what can be done.

These chimneys are, for the most part, small and can be seen to have once occupied a corner. This says "down Mexico way" quite clearly. The Latins are very seldom observed to have built large chimneys and fireplaces. There are hereabouts several raised platforms, stone faced and earth filled, that were once cooking cubicles. Charcoal or dry manzanita was fed into the embrasures under the kettles, draft being obtained by narrow tuyers or apertures at the front. Overhead an inverted funnel constructed of woven brush, plastered smooth with clay, vented smoke and fumes to the outside. This uptake, when lime was available, was always white-washed. This detail is shown in a diorama of a scene taken from Camp O'pera in the museum at Jackson. Sometimes these quadrangles were extended and a hemispherical horno or oven built at one side. An oversize and sophisticated version of this arrangement may be seen in the Mission pozzolera or cocina at Carmel.

This next is entirely conjectural but this is probably one of the places of refuge to which the poor terrified Mexican population fled after the genocidal wave of terrorism at Drytown and Rancheria. That, under those conditions and circumstances, it should be dedicated to the honor of Maria Santissima is certainly understandable.

There are other similar locations and remains in the wilderness of the west face of Bear Mountain and two or three of a like type in the Siberia Range, that being the next ridge to the west of the Bear.

The nearly vertical canyon walls and impenetrable chemise with which they are covered offered a large measure of protection and concealment. We who came long afterward in time hope that it so functioned and well.

Columbia Bar

The bronze plaque facing the penstock controls at the center of Pardee Dam states that the mass of concrete retaining the lake waters rises from the stream center bedrock to a height of 368 feet. Dropping half of the 68 to rise to the probable road and street levels and the other half to follow the average surface level of the lake, we have three hundred feet of water above town center. Thus by a wide margin we come up with the fact that Columbia Bar is the most deeply immersed of all of our long departed settlements. The name itself was probably applied with a patriotic connotation. However we have no confirmation of this from any source.

At the construction of Pardee Dam, in the late twenties, several thousand dollars in coarse gold was taken from the stream bed in the routine clean-up of the foundation. In the recovery were included various pieces of jewelry of gold, coins both silver and gold, Spanish Mexican, American, and South American, Masonic emblems; evidence that more valuables are lost in the ordinary processes of living than is commonly supposed. Evidence also in the retrieved gold that the early miners were far short of getting all of it.

An enormous slab of greenstone, this monolith at a guess being perhaps fifteen feet thick, forty feet wide, and one hundred and twenty feet long some distance from town center capped gravels and earth that were extremely rich.

Sometime before 1860 Chinese miners working under it were recovering so much that they made the fatal error of undermining it to the point that it came down upon them. Thirty five were trapped under that great stone, now three hundred feet down.

By Chinese custom, after years of interment, the bones were taken up and placed in large jars or funerary urns and re-interred until such time as they could be sent home to China. A gold coin was placed in each jar to cover costs of transportation. This custom, when discovered by the whites, brought exactly the reaction that you think. However, when the coin is missing, the fare home is guaranteed by the great and powerful Six Companies of San Francisco's Chinatown. This operation, by no means yet completed, is carried on whenever an old Chinese cemetery is discovered in the Mother Lode. A segment of it was effected before the Chinese cemetery at Camanche was inundated by the rising waters of the lake just two years ago.

Over areas of the abandoned cemeteries, the barrel shaped jars, emptied of their contents may be observed with their tops opened at about a foot below grade. About them for years will cling the fragrance of sandalwood, strips of it having been placed with the bones at the re-interment.

Our sympathies go out to the thirty-five. Their bones will never rest in the good earth of Quan Tung. May their spirits not be too greatly troubled by the Feng Shuey of an alien land.

China Gulch

References to China Gulch in the early accounts are always oblique and incidental to a story of some of the communities adjacent. In terrain it is a gentle sloping plain from which deep gulches are slotted into the surrounding hills. At its outlet to the Mokelumne, it narrows to a width of perhaps 300 yards, sentineled at right and left by bold sandstone mesas, forming, now that inundation has made it a strait, a miniature of the Pillars of Hercules. Its central water course, of which the upper end only is now above shore line, topped out at a saddle of the hills through which a thirty-foot cut brought the Boston Store branch of the Lancaster Ditch to a position from which right and left branches served the placers of both east and west perimeters. High above, at the north, a long redan of the Indian fortress mentioned under Camp O'pera, dominates the scene below. Great additional sight plain is afforded by the tourelle of the Chemisal that functions as an auxiliary guard post to the Buena Vista Peaks to the north-west.

Below the ditches, both east and west, may still be

traced the old beds of penstocks that dropped from them to build the required pressures. Some of the old platforms or bases of the monitors may be made out, facing great spaces of manmade cliffs, in color cream white, the aggregate blown from them having long ago tumbled across the riffles of the sluice boxes.

The little valley was, at center, the most entirely unexpected thing in some ways to be encountered in the whole area. Going downstream one came to a flat, almost at the exact center. A screen of live oak, when penetrated, disclosed a long wide lane, in length easily a statute mile. At right and left the lane was bounded by walls of almost spherical cobblestone. Now here the entirely unusual; these walls were a flattened pyramid in section, perhaps five feet thick at the base, a batter of perhaps a foot on each face terminating at a height of five feet in a three foot wide top. At intervals of a half block or less, openings were left, of the width of a narrow street, the wall ends at each side being raised and rounded off in a pylon eighteen inches or two feet above the wall height. In the embrasures were some scant evidence that there once existed wooden structures, though it was hard to be sure. The lane, walls, openings all were shaded by a double row of enormous oaks. Coming upon this out of the surrounding wilderness in the blazing heat of mid-Summer gave one the eerie sensation of having by some inadavertence moved bodily into a tale out of the Arabian Nights.

In endless repetition, in an endeavor to tell the story of these ancient things, one uncovers more stories that defy explanation or decipherment than one tells. Like the above; What are Spanish walls, right off of the windy plain of La Mancha, doing in a Chinese community? To the best of my information this particular pattern of wall is found nowhere else in the Mother Lode. Who knows? I do not.

This may be as good a time as any for a few remarks

upon the Chinese habitations, their dimensions, materials, and methods of construction. Examples near the placers in China Gulch, Arroyo Negro, below Camp O'pera, and along lower Dry Creek are in substantial agreement. Here it is: in a hillside bearing a gradient of thirty per cent or close thereto, a rectangle of from sixteen to twenty feet on a side was staked out, the hill being preferably of dense clay or soft sandstone. Excavation was then carried out, which, when completed, gave full head room at the rear. Any material available for masonry was then used to run up the front wall, a door opening provided in the exact center, two board shuttered windows were worked into the two triangular walls at each side. These were small. At the rear upgrade a deep V trench drained away the water of the rains.

At floor level, inside, no great effort was needed to excavate a fireplace into the back wall and bring it to operational level. Two methods of doing this are still observable, from identified ruins. In one, the fire box is capped by a wide thin slab of serpentine and the chimney dug behind it through the earth and rimmed with stone against the entrance of water at grade level outside. In the alternate, a fourteen-inch diameter miner's pipe was acquired, together with a piece of sheet iron. The pipe was inletted into the back wall to flush, or approximately, and its surplus length, perhaps sixteen feet, carried the smoke high and away and afforded good draft. The sheet iron at the bottom made an excellent stove and truly flat surface for cooking. The last was obviously the setup of a group that had good joss and very probably such a place was the abode of Ho Tei the god of happiness.

Union Bar

As nearly as may be determined Union Bar was completely obliterated in the great flood and inundation of the early Sixties that destroyed Poverty Bar, Put's Bar, and erased all traces of human occupancy in a dozen riverside communities.

What we may dredge up must come from the written and printed page. Of this the most informative material comes from numerous references in the *Sacramento Bee* to consignments of Springfield rifles, minie ball, powder, and military equipment of every type in use at that time, sent to the Union Guards of Union Bar. Research in the State Library at Sacramento, the Huntington Library at San Marino, and the Bancroft Library at Berkeley might give us some light on this organization. What we have upon it here is essentially nothing.

This company and its requisite *materiel* presupposes an armory and arsenal. There are, in contemporary news briefs, references tantalizingly short, to such buildings. A thing that might help, if it were available, would be a look into the State's military archives that would tell us why Union Bar was selected as the base of a militia unit over the competition of Lancha Plana, Poverty Bar and Put's Bar; each a thriving, populous, and agressive community.

In the process of building the Pardee Dam, the buckets of the machinery loading gravel and sand into the cars of the highline monorail uncovered a whole grid of stub masonry walls of a thickness of two and one half to three feet. This was on the river's north bank. At the time it was conjectured that this was Union Bar. It probably was.

Of anything tangible and physical of this place we have about as much as we have of King Arthur's Land of Lyoness or of Plato's Atlantis.

We know for a certainty that hundreds of miners toiled here and wrote letters to loved ones far distant. Some one of these letters we may hope to someday find, that will give us more information and a shaft of light into what is now mostly darkness.

We do not know how much weight the Union Guards placed in the scales, but we do know that it was one component that kept California on the side of the Union.

Put's Bar

The strike at Put's Bar was made by one Putnam, later, for many years, a resident of Ione. Several hundred men worked here, of which it is chronicled that many of them were Chinese. The bar being immediately below the point at which China Gulch debouches into the Mokelumne, this can not come as too much of a surprise.

When some of the miners turned to agricultural and horticultural pursuits, they found that the soil of California could be generous indeed. The melons, grapes, peaches, and apricots of the bar were a wonder for miles around.

Its claim to fame can rest upon its possession of the Butler Claim in entire security. In telling the story of the riches of this network of communities around Lancha Plana, the charge of exaggeration can easily be laid.

Of the Butler Claim let us let Mason tell it. Remember at the time of writing, many of the actors in the play were very much alive and he had the benefit of personal interviews with them. Within these brackets here it is verbatim:

The Butler claim was situated at the foot of the deep gorge which came out of the mountains and was first owned by a party of negroes; hence was called the Nigger Claim. The river was dammed and turned, as usual in river claims. The channel was straight and smooth and offered no holding place for the gold, and all of the party, except Butler, left the claim. The following year Butler borrowed five or six hundred dollars of Uncle Pompey, another colored man, and opened the claim a little lower down in a bend. It proved the richest piece of ground ever found in the vicinity, or even in the two counties, being a mass of gravel six or eight feet deep, literally lousy with gold. A day's work with a rocker would produce ten, twenty, thirty, and even fifty thousand dollars. Fred Westmoreland, a cool and sensible person, not liable to be excited, says he frequently saw a milk pan, the ordinary gold pan, heaping full for a day's work, so full that it could not be lifted by the rim without tearing in pieces. Some of the dust, not so rich, was washed in a long tom. According to Tom Love a hundred dollars worth of dust could be seen following the dirt along the sluice box, the hands who were tending it stealing the dust by the handful. A face or breast was worked on the bed of gravel and the gold showed from the top to the bottom, a distance of six or eight feet. At the bottom, pure dust could be gathered with a spoon. When it was known how immeasurably rich it was a number of men were anxious to have a share. The former partners' of Butler were hunted up and induced to sell interests in the claim. A number of suits were commenced against Butler and and some half-dozen or more lawyers engaged to share the proceeds if successful. A receiver was appointed to take charge of the claim, pending the suits. Robert Bennett, known as Bob Bennet, a well known citizen of Lancha Plana was once appointed custodian for a day. In a few pansful of dirt he obtained dust to the amount of two thousand, two hundred dollars, which he, "Damned fool that I was, I turned over to the court. Everybody was taking and keeping all that they could get." It was too much for the old man. He was taken sick with fever and shortly died. It was known by his friends that he had some eighty thousand dollars in deposit at Mokelumne Hill, as much or more at Sacramento, and also immense sums buried in unknown spots. The public administrator took possession of the property and there was not enough found to pay a few small outstanding debts.

Comment on the above is just not possible.

Fort Ann

Local tradition asserts that Fort Ann was brought into being by the stationing here of twenty men of the U.S. Army, a commissioned officer and one or two sergeants. We may well believe that in a very short time they all deserted to go mining; this the second part of the tradition.

There were rich outcroppings of paralleling veins of the East Lode directly beneath the site of the fort itself. Surface scars and old shaft openings bear witness to extensive operations. An old arrastre close to a vein of exposed quartz still possesses its drag stones. The Fort Ann Mine and the Posey Mine, both being ventures of considerable substance, operated until the early years of the twentieth century.

The outlines of the log barracks, headquarters, and stables may still be traced. A flat-topped cone of stone near a corner of the headquarters building held, until a few years ago, the base of the flagpole. Close at hand a flat meadow of perhaps five acres was used as a parade ground. We do not seem to have a scrap of information leading to the origin of the name. Fort Ann is the commonly accepted version though a few early references to it label it Fort Anna.

Arkansas Ferry

References to Arkansas Ferry, in the earliest accounts, are fairly numerous. The place is firmly established upon maps available in the mid-fifties including that of John Doble. The road leading to it is easily traceable, on both the Calaveras and Amador side, though Doble's map does not show the culverts, masonry supports, and riprap on the lower side, that appear in the approaches at the Morrow and Westmoreland bridges. Fairly solid evidence here that it antedated them, and was, perhaps, the earliest visible crossing above the original Lancha Plana.

Its site is a place of considerable charm. A half circle of cliffs on the south is matched by almost identical formations on the north: the whole forming a deep bowl in the bottom of which the Mokelumne forms a small lake with enough current at most seasons of the year to power a gravity ferry.

The road snaked a tortuous course down the gorge of the river to the south landing. On the north side it spiraled and looped past a ledge or bench, of some acres in extent, that apparently was the townsite, to a point where it cleared the north rim of the canyon.

On the Amador side, an islet in quadrilateral outline of perhaps fifty by one hundred yards, was the footing of an eight room house, constructed of stratified serpentine laid in adobe, to which the white lime plaster adhered for many years. Not too striking in appearance when viewed horizontally, it was quite impressive in its open-to-the-sky gauntness when observed from a needle like projection of the north rim. Who built it and why will probably never be known.

As of this writing the islet and the building are gone, some small fragments of the east end excepted. One of our recurring floods sometime in the last forty years, has obliterated almost every trace. Just at random, if one tried to pick out the one that swept it away, it may have been the great catastrophe of the year 1955 that, among its other acts of destruction, wiped out Yuba City.

Contreras

John Doble, among his other talents, a cartographer of no small ability considering the means at his disposal, places Contreras at about a half mile north of the north fork of the Mokelumne. Now a map published in 1866, and released by the Government subsequent to the first surveys of this terrain, locates the town at river's edge, beneath the arch or loop of the old wagon road to West Point. The new road appears to follow the line of the old quite closely.

A synthesis of these two is easily attained when we turn to the old records, which informs us that the town held a population of from 1500 to 2000, along a fold of the ravine from the locale of the Defender Mine right down to the river. Both maps are correct then, subject only to where town center is placed.

No very useful purpose would be served by an attempt to plot the street lines after more than a century of cutting new logging roads, logging out the last of the virgin forest, cutting fire breaks, and again logging the second growth. The use of the masonry buildings as a source of dimensional stone for other structures cut deep into the remnants of the town as early as fifty or sixty years ago.

To give a bit from personal memory, much steatite or soapstone was removed from the fireplaces and walls in the early years of this century. This material was even more attractive than the old hand-made and clamp burned brick; besides being serviceable in any place that brick would function, it appealed to whatever was latent in the artistic ability of would be sculptors. Its soap-like texture is readily amenable to cutting tools of a type used in wood carving. There is probably not even a scrap remaining at the site at this time.

The water powered arrastre drew the attention of the early observers. They state that the ditches from the Mokelumne supplied the moving force. No photograph of one of them seems to exist. Were they overshot or undershot wheels At a guess they were probably overshot, in that the flumes could deliver water to them at the top, which was the most efficient method. Bevel gears would have to have been employed for the transmission of power. Whether these were ordered from foundries in the East, or, more probably, England, or were wooden aflairs, cut from the native black locust or heart madrone we may someday find out.

The ore worked was crystalline and sugar quartz of great richness; obtained from shafts that at a depth of around fifty feet could no longer be worked by reason of encountering water in excessive amounts. These primitive mills yielded returns of several thousand dollars per day from each unit.

We go now to the printed page to learn of the great dance hall that stood at the south end of the town, used by amateur thespians in some sort of what, by our parlance, could be termed little theatre operations. Strolling players of professional standing also made it a port of call.

This edifice was built and operated by the founder of the town, Senor Contreras, and was the scene of grand balls and revues; presided over by his lady and his beautiful daughters. Repeated references are extant, and from mutually supporting sources, affirming the beauty and grace of the distaff side of the family, and the high moral character of the entire unit. One comes upon this statement of fact again and again, like a golden thread in a silk tapestry. This is the more remarkable when seen against the black backdrop of the eviction of the settlers from the Arroyo Seco, the Rancheria Massacre, the murdering terrorism perpetrated upon the peaceful Mexican population, and the boiling hatreds and prejudices not yet cooled from the Mexican War. The family was held in well deserved affectionate regard and was even accorded a measure of respect by the rowdy and turbulent elements of the community.

In 1965, in the month of July, the fair at Sonora, in our neighboring County of Tuolumne was presided over by Senor Luis Encinas the Governor of the State of Sonora of our Sister Republic.

The theme and motif of the Fair was that of according honor to the Mexican founder of the town, who gave it the name of their beloved state. With His Excellency and visiting dignitaries came a band, Los Mariachias Coculas. Once again the streets of Sonora vibrated to the pulsating fire of Latin music.

Persons well along in years, whose grandparents endured the rigors of the passage of the Camino del Diablo and the Journado del Muerto, came down from the hills to reactivate Spanish learned at Mother's knee, and rusty from long disuse.

Of the many taproots from which we have grown there are those that run high onto the Plateau and right into Tenochititlan. Here was moisture again being applied to those taproots. May they grow and expand.

In this small account alloted to Contreras, we have as good a place as any to pay tribute to our Mexican pioneers. When we apportion honors to each group and segment whose blood, sweat, and endurance built what we have today, we can be sure that there are none higher or more numerous than those honors that may properly be accorded the Sons of Anahuac.

Slabtown

The very early fifties constituted the time bracket in which Huffaker's Mill supplied the material which both created and named Slabtown. In the absence of any old ambrotype that would give us an idea of the town's appearance we may acquire a general impression from a scanning of Charles Nahl's painting "Sunday Morning in the Mines." Here are the green mill slabs nailed to round poles, the bark starting to peel from both where weathered at the edges: Window and door openings screened by the canvas stripped from the yards of tall ships after their ordeal of the Horn; picked clean of every usable thing and abandoned to rot in row upon row in the tide flats below Montgomery Street; the perfect illustration of what Bayard Taylor termed so aptly, "the rude and unlovely architecture of the early fifties."

In the ensuing years substantial buildings were erected, the town, in the transformation, assuming the look of its neighboring communities. Out of any listing of distinguished citizens emerging from the ebb, flow, and eddies of the swirling early population, a substantial segment were domiciled in, or at one time, residents of Slabtown.

In 1905 a great forest and brush fire leveled much of the town. The rest in the intervening years fell into complete ruin and disappeared.

The environs of Slabtown and the country at, and east of, the Lode still bears the imprint, though it has mostly been neglected or destroyed, of the skill and energy of the early Italian immigrants. They came, many of them, in 49, and in the years immediately following. We owe them a debt that not only we cannot repay, but probably not even fully comprehend.

Quite soon men from Italy looked up from the sluice boxes and arrastres and saw the deep red earth, the sloping hillsides, and a hot sun in a cobalt sky. In all essentials they observed this was quite like their own Terra Bella and they were not long in doing something about it. The slopes were terraced and planted to Zinfandel and Mission grapes and to all varieties usable for wine and table and in the production of raisins.

The small streams were dammed and diverted to gardens. Olive, almond, English walnut, fig, pear, nectarine, cherry, apricot, apple, just about every known fruit tree was planted and brought to production by highly skilled and sympathetic hands. In an incredibly short period of time, a far frontier, affording at best a meagre diet, was converted to a gourmet's paradise. To this day, there are renowned dining places, in the Mother Lode, whose Italian cuisine is flattered by attempts at imitation; country wide. And their roots are way back there.

In horse-powered days, some of the predecessors of these famed establishments operated at roadside, to the great boon of teamsters of the long jerk lines, passing drummers with full sample cases on the rear flats of the buckboards, cow men pushing their herds to the Sierra meadows in summer and returning in autumn, and just the passing public in general.

A typical layout: Above a slanted stone wall back of the hitching racks a large dining room mostly glass sided; and shaded old olive trees. At the rear, the cooking space; a large kettle of minestrone asimmer on the great range. On a sort of great butcher's block, dry sausages of many kinds, fat red onions, home cured olives, varieties of cheeses, a great circle of sour Italian bread. All of this from the good earth hard by. The bread: from the outdoor horno on the hill above. By a few passes of the large knife at hand, sandwiches of unbelievable savor were created.

In the stone wall close to the kitchen, an arched doorway led to the cold bodega deep in the heart of the mountain. Here were rows of oaken casks aging the wines, salamis in pendant **stalactites** completing their cure, cheeses: provolone, swiss, and parmesano mellowing to perfection. Shelving held spices, a most essential part of the magic of these places. From town; cans of whole peppercorns, alspice, and cardamon, from the landscaped herb garden edging the stone paved entrance; savory, oregano, coriander, basil, and rosemary in square faced apothecary jars. Will anyone ever have it so good again?

Some part of what was lovingly created so long ago may still be seen if one cares to drive up the ridge road from Sutter Hill to New York Ranch, passing the vineyards and orchards. Another tour affording a glance into the past on any one of the roads that wind through the Shenandoah Valley; coming out at the vineyards and winery of D'Agostini. Here, the edifice of the winery, built of cut stone and great adzed and mortised timbers, bears the bronze medallion attached by the State of California to historic buildings.

In the tap room a glass faced cabinet displays medals won for excellence of product at expositions and fairs. The beautifully kept vineyards on the hill give point to Virgil's dictum that "Bacchus loves the hillsides."

If we may, let us have a look at the tool or implement that was first used in bringing all of this into being, the *saupa*. This double toothed or bladed hand cultivator, wielded by the hard-muscled, turned and aerated the soil much deeper than any plow. It was capable of being used in tight places, and around rock outcroppings, where plow cultivation was impossible. Whether there are any of them around any more is a question. When quite young the writer saw many of them in use, and, as is always the case of that which is commonplace, did not notice them at all. At school, our Latin Reader contained a series of frames taken from that spiral cartoon strip on the column of Trajan in Rome. There were the enduring Roman colonists, bridging the rivers, laying the roads, raising the buildings—but mostly swinging the saupa, planting vine and fruit trees, bringing light, law, order, and culture to the barbarian space soon to be metamorphised into Dacia Felix. This scene could have been taken from our own locale, or vice versa.

This inanimate object rates a place in the museum case bearing the label, "Tools that made the West" alongside of the Kentucky rifle, the Winchester, the Colt Revolver, the Hudson Bay Ax, the Framing Adz, the Froe, the Grain Cradle, the Flail, the Branding Iron, the Rawhide Reata, to mention but a few of its peers.

So nice if some latter day Keats or Shelley would come forward and write an ode to the saupa; a basic tool of civilization over five continents and three milennia.

106

Italian Saloons

At some point in this narrative may we insert a few words upon the Italian Saloons of the Mother Lode. They were, always, housed in one of those structures of massive stone from the skilled hands of the Italian masons and quarrymen. We are fortunate in that many of them are still around and in various kinds of usage to this day. Two excellent examples are the Amasa Building and the Ghilieri Building both at Jackson Gate.

Their thick walls and stone paved interiors held an ocean of cold air to which entry from the blazing heat of a summer afternoon was a delight that was just unimaginable.

Tables and chairs for the use of small groups across the expanse of pavement were sometimes of conventional pattern, though the old California type of chair, that of the woven rawhide bottom and slat ladderback, were much in use. Alternately; a slab adzed from a great log of oak, legs of the same material split, rounded, and with their ends inserted into auger holes in the slab. Here we have a tavola in the pre-renaissance mold. The seats for this unit are *scabellos* and *panchettos* roughed out in a like manner, the material most generally heart madrone.

The great bar, a polished expanse of walnut, was balanced right and left of the mirror by rack on rack of imported liqueurs and brandies the listing of which would serve no purpose. On each wing, bronze hooped cooperage held local wines and brandies that, in their excellence, could well meet any competition.

At center, atop the mirror, a scale model of the monument to Victor Emmanuel in Rome. An alternate;

a miniature in bronze of Romulus, Remus, and the she-wolf from the Capitoline in Rome.

On a niche in the stone wall, or in the depths of an embrasured window, a bust portraying the sour visage of Dante Alighieri, this I believe a copy of an original by Donatello; alternately might be seen, to mention one or two of a number, Caesar Augustus or Flavius Vespasianus. These were not the cold of lifeless marble but of tinted flesh and draperies, in the classical tradition.

On the walls there were always two pictures or rather three; two of them matching, one of Victor Emmanuel and the other of Conti di Cavour. The third, and this of the same size or a bit larger, the fiery red mane and curled Babylonian beard of Guiseppi Garibaldi.

These interiors were illuminated at nightfall by lamps that were probably the products of the quarries of Carrara. The Italians, of that time and of right now, were and are well knowledged of the sorcery of light filtered through thin panes of marble. It may well be that these things just mentioned are treasured heirlooms of some of the old families residing within the county.

Of passing interest were the large calendars distributed by firms exporting art goods, delicacies, and liquors from the Ligurian Coast.

Let us try to dredge up two of them from memory.

One: Carthaginians off Cape Mylae in complete disarray collecting their lumps from the trireme-bourne marines of Caius Duilius the Consul.

Two: Genovese galleasses, in the line ahead, forcing entrance to the Bay of Tunis, past the guarding forts on the headlands, their hot cannon pouring death and dismemberment into the serried ranks of Turk and Barbary Corsair packed on the decks of the enemy fleet.

On the carosse of the flagship in the foreground, his armor and morion a rippling irridescence of polished steel, niello, and gold inlay, the bane and nemesis of the infidel Solyman's Caputan Pasha stands, sword in hand, directing the fight. He is the greatest—if we except Columbus—of all the Genoese admirals who ruled the salt seas, the one and only Andrea Doria. There is our saloon. Shall we try for a bit of animation? It is Saturday night. Hundreds of men have surfaced from depths of more than a mile, turning the work at the drift faces over to the incoming shift. Three or four experts on the accordion assemble on the low platform at one corner, the light dancing on the shells of the instruments, a mass of polished silver. The crash, rumble, and roar of the stamps of the Kennedy and Argonaut mines are, for a time, slightly muted by a shift of wind to the North that brings the sound of the Oneida and South Eureka, dulled by distance.

A tentative run over the keys and the orchestra is off with six or a dozen tenor and basso voices in support. Let us ask them for three numbers that they know so well: La Spagnola, Santa Lucia, Torno a Sorrento.

Pokerville

It is amazing to contemplate how much time and effort is expended upon creating a mystery out of something that is quite forthright, A case in point: The name of Pokerville that some writers have endeavored to twist to Puckerville Pakerville, or whatever.

There were enough settlers nearby whose descendants may still be located not too far from there that can and will tell why the name was given.

In the Winter of the great flood of 1850, 1851 the

stormbound miners fought boredom and shack fever with interminable sessions of poker—beans, buttons, and various small objects being used in lieu of chips.

Over the years, there have been several notices taken, in the press, of the old building that stands at town edge —asserted to have once been a stage depot. Among numerous claimants to such status, this one could have been authentic. The old timbers supporting the roof and the stone wall at the back have been in position much longer than a century. How these timbers, completely exposed to the elements, have lasted so long is inexplicable. They were adzed and broadaxed square, fitted together with mortise, tenon, and hardwood pegs. As various books on carpentry have stated, this is not just the old method of construction; it is the best.

At the south rim of the little flat of Pokerville, Indian Creek drops precipitously into a deep ravine. At the funnel mouth of its descent, the little walled dam, tail race, and wheel mounts, all constructed of cut and mortared greenstone, are all that remains of the De Augostine Flouring Mill. This was a large grist mill, built, at a guess, in the 1860's or 1870's, that stood for many years at the side of the narrow road where it enters the canyon. It was in place in 1914, had disappeared by the early twenties. Another guess: It was probably torn down in 1916 or 1917. One cannot contemplate the complete disappearance of all that once made a landscape so charming and completely individualized, without feeling depressed. Our once delightful countryside is rapidly deteriorating into God's Own Junkyard.

For years, exploration of the platforms, runways, decks, and darkened passageways around the deserted machinery was an adventure for juveniles and those in search of the entirely unusual.

The grain went in by conveyor to the top floor and ended as flour at roadside, in a warehouse of fair capacity. In between, long levers of hardwood shifted

110

the power from belt conveyors to grinders, to winnowing machinery, and to whatever was necessary in the operation of milling, much of it, of course, beyond the comprehension of the casual visitor. Bottomside, an oversize wheel-and-screw mechanism moved the flood gates that controlled the admission of water to the 12 foot, undershot, water wheel.

Somewhere there has to be a photograph of this old mill. When and if ever it is discovered the first reaction to viewing it will be that it is either a shot taken of a set produced by a crew on the Paramount Lot or the product of the brush of an artist in the employ of Hallmark Greeting Cards. A thing can be too perfect to gain credibility. The case with this.

Across the road, directly in front, wide stones steps, flanked by curving retaining walls of stone plastered white and guarded at each side by two tall funereal-looking cypresses, lead to empty space that once must have been taken up by a home of some considerable importance. Whatever was here has been entirely gone for perhaps all of the years of this century. Whoever built and whoever demolished never paid the least attention to the ground upon which they were working. A hard rain or just the twist of a boot toe will expose beads, some of these bearing the monogram of the Czarina Catherine. Charcoal and tiny fragments of bone give evidence that this was, perhaps for uncounted centuries, a spot where cremation was performed by the Maidu.

Here again we are at another impasse between the written account and the intrinsic evidence of the ground. The north boundary of the Miwok and the southern boundary of the Maide is given by all authorities as the Cosumnes. In disposal of the dead the Miwok practised inhumation, the Maide, cremation. This site is several miles south of the Cosumnes. There is another identifying factor: the mounds of the Miwok, while they contain some beads, are plentifully supplied with ornaments of

111

haliotis and abalone shell. In contrast, the Maidu ran heavily to beads, both of primitive manufacture and those acquired in trade with the whites.

Wasn't it Heinrich Schliemann who said, "When the written record and that uncovered by the spade are in conflict take that of the spade"? We do.

From a squirrel hole at this site many years ago the writer removed a metal ax head. It was small, somewhere in heft between a tomahawk and a Hudson Bay tommy ax. It bore a crest, meaningless at the time. Long since misplaced or stolen its likeness may be seen in the museum at Coliseum Park in Los Angeles. It is there identified as trade goods of the Russian-American Fur Trading Company and the crest is its trademark.

Little if any notice has been taken by historians of the extent of the contacts, trade, and, perhaps, cultural of the Russian presence in California with the natives.

Vallejo in his memoirs makes the statement that by the year 1790 the Promyscheliniki had exterminated the beaver in the streams running into the Sacramento and the San Joaquin. But says he: by the year 1800 the Soldados de Cuera had exterminated the Promyscheliniki.

The chronicles are emphatic in informing us that Fort Ross was founded in 1812. From where did these trappers materialize two decades and more, before they possessed a supply base or a staging area?

Can it possibly be that some ruins of a pattern apparently incompatible with what we know to be of American, Spanish, or Mexican source that are found in the Lode are the shelters, trading posts or bases of a past, mid-eighteenth century long, thrust south from Sitka by the Muscovites?

Here we are just about at par for the whole course. In an attempt to answer two or three small questions we have uncovered several large ones to which we have no answer.

Jacalitos

In our series of ghost town sites every one except this can be pinpointed and placed upon the map with something approximating accuracy. In the case of Jacalitos not so. No individual survives nor is there anything documentary that gives us a bit of help in nailing it to an exact spot. The old accounts and newspapers, time after time, in reporting some misdeed or act of violence, refer to it as Jacalitos near the Q Ranch. It appears to have escaped notice completely, aside from that of being mentioned as a base or staging area for the commission of some criminal act. As is noted elsewhere, the perpetrators of the massacre at Lower Rancheria were first reported at Jacalitos.

It must have disappeared before 1860. Otherwise some legend or folktale giving its location would have come down to the turn of the century.

Now to indulge in pure conjecture as to where it might have been: let us note that the headquarters of the Q Ranch stood on the south side of the road. The position of this part of the road has not changed in more than a century. The ranch buildings were on an average three hundred yards west of the present highway bridge and on the south side. Upstream from the bridge, a distance of from an eighth to a half mile, there are extensive dredger tailing hummocks, certain evidence of gold-bearing ground. The dredges recovered those values not reached by the sluices. This way well have been the site.

One final note: As of this day, live oak on the banks and ash trees in the watercourse grow in profusion. In the building of a jacal, long-shanked live oak brush and ash poles for the swais or binder strips are preferred material. Certainly then and now it was close at hand.

From the use of the diminutive (itos) we may well infer that they were small.

Chaparral Hill

Here in February in 1853 was formed the organization that later, expanding and metamorphising into the California Rangers, terminated the career of Murrieta's band of outlaws at the Arroyo Cantova. The founders of this were Jeff Gatewood, John Hall, Sam Davis, and Peter Woodbeck, under the leadership of Deputy Sheriff Ellis. They and members of their posse were soon tested in battle, right at Chaparral Hill. Greatly outnumbered they were forced to retreat to a ravine at the bottom of the hill at which point they were able to mount and ride to Mokelumne Hill.

The day following, at the Phoenix Quartz Mill, the caretaker and Peter Woodbeck were killed by Murrieta and Three Fingered Jack. Of the outlaw band; Juan Sanchez carried a wound to Camp O'pera, where he was hung by the posse of Sheriff Clark, as is noted in the bit on that town. Others of the group, several of them wounded, dispersed to Capulope, Greaserville, and Yaqui Camp on the Calaveras side.

If anyone is interested in following the twists, zigzags, and spirals of this blood splattered trail, he is referred to Walter Noble Burns's most excellent book "The Robin Hood of El Dorado" which is documented most thoroughly and was five years in preparation.

Three or four stout footings of greenstone, the upper portions most likely removed by one of the recurring floods were still visible on the slope above the river before the lake filled. These showed a wall height of three to four feet, in those spots where transverse dikes of bedrock shielded them from the current during inundations. All of the above of course presently deep under.

On the crest, after several strata of soil were removed in succession, those patient gleaners of the 1860's and 1870's, the Chinese took over. Several of their small dwellings of conglomerate mud-mortared rock are still there as of 1965.

There must have been a reason for the appellation "Chaparral Hill." What it supports now is a thicket of digger pine that, growing inside as well as outside of the wall enclosures, throws the whole scene into deep shade.

The boundary between Lancha Plana and Chaparral Hill seems to have been an almost imaginary line, something like that between Oakland and Berkeley or Chicago and Gary. Yet all surviving records maintain a clear and sharp distinction in any references to either settlement.

Sometime in the early 1850's, it would appear, it was discovered that the river was more easily crossed at a higher elevation, which resulted in the, at least partial, abandonment of the original Lancha Plana or flat boat. In sequence we read of Judge Palmer's Bridge, Delaney's Bridge, Westmoreland's Ferry, and the Westmoreland Bridge. All of these thrust out from Chaparral Hill. Of Judge Palmer's Bridge: this disappeared in a raging flood while his honor was engrossed in a game of cards. When informed that it had just vanished, the judge calmly queried, "What is your bid gentlemen"? Of Delaney's Bridge we have very little except that it followed that of the judge in a flood, a season or so later. The Westmoreland Ferry could not have been in existence more than a year or two, as it was replaced by the Westmoreland Bridge in 1856. This, perhaps the most magnificent and photogenic of all of the suspension bridges of the gold rush, stood until 1964, one-hundred and eight years. At around 1900 the floor was torn up. One by one the cross stringers rotted. The great cables and pendant wire ropes endured. Each of the four pylon cable supports were composed in turn of four oak timbers 24 inches square twenty feet long, not any one containing an observable pin knot. The trees from which these were cut must have been well worth seeing. Dressed stone laid at the faces and footings was outclassed only by the ruins of a stone structure, built around the year 1870, to implement an irrigation project utilizing the waters of the Mokelumne. This was perhaps a hundred yards downstream from the bridge and appeared to be as though a section of the Great Wall of China had been picked up and dropped to the bedrock. Never utilized, the twenty foot thick masonry was breached by the Old Mok in a raging Winter Flood and the whole project was abandoned after the expenditure of one hundred thousand dollars.

At the south terminal of the dam, the handsome coursed stone work of the outlet control gates, now fifty feet under, should endure for untold centuries. In the dam itself the work could be correctly termed cyclopean. The individual stones, weighing tons each, cut, fit, and mortared with high precision. The professionals that turned in this score were not exceeded in competence anywhere on earth.

While on the subject of bridges two additional that were thrown across the Mokelumne should be worth our attention. The maps on file at the office of the County Recorder show both the Westmoreland and the Morrow Bridges as being in existence in the year 1866.

The masonry approaches, header walls, and road grades of the Morrow are still plainly in view to anyone afloat in the canyon who goes above the new highway bridge and the mouth of Oregon Gulch. We have no clue as to what material was used in the span. On the evidence of the width and height it might be reasonable to suppose that it may have been an arch or cantilever of timber. Subsequent research disclosed, upon the evidence of a map dated 1866, that it was a suspension bridge.

A few hundred yards above this, the cliffs soar upward to a spire on both the north and south rims. Here, at the apexes, may be viewed the remanants of the most daring engineering project of the olden time—the spanning of the river. All of the cliff supporting the roadway approach at the south has fallen. Half of the north approach has likewise disappeared. The cables that held it aloft are draped over the north headwall and hang perpendicularly into the waters of the lake. Much of the timber supports, thoroughly rotten but still recognizable, remain at the north pier together with the attendant iron work. As this is written, plans are afoot to lower the two great iron caps that were guides and stress supports for the cables down to a barge and remove them to the lake museum.

The cables are of the type described at the Lamb Bridge at Copper Hill, of the Westmoreland, and of others in the early bridges of the Lode. By tradition they all came from England. There appears to be no reason to doubt this.

Anyone viewing the remnants of this ancient suspension opus—for which we, incidentally, do not have a name—can readily grasp that crossing it must have given a real thrill, The expression "cliff hanger" is here no figure of speech.

For the story of how all of this came to ruin we must draw upon legend which is that at the time of the battle of Chaparral Hill; Joaquin Valenzuela, Murrieta's transportation officer, collapsed it accidentally by running a band of horses over it. Since the battle occurred in February 1853 the bridge could not have been in existence any length of time and its period of service could not possibly have exceeded a few months.

The yellowing pages of the *Lancha Plana Prospect* carry advertisements of the mercantile firms of J. W. D.

117

Palmer and Co.—could it be our friend the imperturbable judge?—John Cook, and William Cook, the latter most probably the owner of the store moved to Buena Vista.

To the miners of Chaparral Hill were awarded the honor of driving a tunnel clear under Alum Peak, out to the China Gulch face. There is no record that it netted them a dime. Perhaps they just liked mining.

It cannot be said that the mineral resources of the place are exhausted. The spine or ridge north of the old road to Lancha Plana is currently being exploited for its deposits of chert, a hard brilliantly green stone much in use as a roof covering.

Old Chaparral Hill if opened to public visit by the park authorities will show all that is remaining thereabouts of the old communities. What has lasted is honest work, and if not too greatly abused should endure for a long time.

Winter's Bar

It would be nice to know and for sure if Winter's Bar received its name from Winter, of the partnership of Kaiser and Winter, who built the ferry at Lancha Plana. John Doble and other cartographers place it upon the map at least as early as 1851 and there are references to it as early as 1850. If it is ever established one way or another it will be, most likely, as so often is the case, by a kind of accident or a variety or inadvertence in which the fact will be uncovered in the act of delving into some other facet of the history of that time.

Recently, in discussions with members of the Historical Society of Calaveras, several of the descendants of people who were residents of the Bar in the 1850's made the statement; and this from a number of different individuals, that there was an *embarcadero* at Winter's Bar. If this be true, and it may well have been, surely this must have been the bitter upper limit of navigation. There are rapids just a few hundred yards above this. They were a bit of quiet water before the lake extended to these parts. Should one grant the authenticity of the above, a surmise might be permitted that this perilous piece of pilotage was first performed by the owners and operators of the pioneer steamer "Pert". It was they who first made the run to Lockford and Clements. A standard history of San Joaquin County tells us that the little vessel ended its career in a boiler explosion and that the skeleton of the hull lies at bankside, in that segment of the Mokelumne at about the middle of its course through the Rancho la Lomita.

A most enduring stone building at the Bar retained for many a year evidence of a use of rawhide that escaped listing in the prologue. This was a roof or as far as could be ascertained from the remnants a sort of skylight. At various of the California Missions there are on exhibit windows of rawhide, and, as may be observed, their pearl translucency passes an amazing amount of light. It is just unbelievable that hide, de-haired, de-membraned, and, of course, well tallowed, could have endured in direct exposure to the weather for a century, but it did.

Yeomet

It is difficult to comprehend how a town—of the size that the old records assert occupied this space—could have been squeezed into the scant dimensions at the bottom of the gorge formed by the confluence of the north and middle forks of the Cosumnes and Big Indian Creek.

The large mercantile establishments of Simpson Beebee & Co., Broman and Co. and others handling all kinds of merchandise were housed in the usual masonry structures, massive in form, iron-doored and iron-shuttered of window, and constituted a solidly built downtown area.

This whole space was attacked and ground sluiced, as returns from the outlying gulches diminished. The buildings were demolished and their footings worked to a depth of many feet.

The printed page makes reference to a large Mexican population in the mid-fifties, and of a sticky period of great tension and stress at a time just subsequent to the Rancheria massacre and the ensuing riots and disorders. Fortunately, very few overt acts of violence are reported and the tensions were gradually lessened.

In a sort of incongrous balance or counterpoise, we are informed that the other population group was composed in a large part of miners from Pennsylvania and mainly from the area of Pittsburgh. They were said to be struck by the fancied resemblance of the place to the confluence of the Alleghany and the Monangahela, where the Ohio takes its beginning. Their imaginations must have really been working overtime if this be so. Were any of them around now it would be most interesting to see where they would park even a scale model of the Golden Triangle.

The town Yeomet is asserted to be taken from the Miwok tongue and is, by translation, rocky falls, this in reference to the up-stream rapids of the Cosumnes. This must have been the extreme northern extension of the Miwok language and culture, as by all anthropoligists' reckonings the Cosumnes is placed as the line of demarcation between Miwok and Maidu.

Of this town we have left just one thing: a cemetry. When last seen it was quite impressive in its live oak shaded isolation at the bottom of the canyon. A perimeter wall of cut, neatly fitted and mortared stone, topped by lacy black English ironwork, gives it definition and aptness. The marking gravestones are in good taste and charming in their quiet simplicity. Some date back to the fifties but a surprising number are in the 1870's and 1880's and many of them bear the crest of the Masonic Order. Even at this period of time, which is far back in our thinking the town, as such, had long since ceased to be.

This illustrates a practice that is by no means abandoned right in our time. These old cemeteries outlived their towns and many of them are still in use. Many persons, then and now, and doubtless will in the future, express a wish which is often carried out, that their mortal remains return to the good earth of the scene of their trials, triumphs, and tribulations.

Within the decade ahead the Nashville Dam is scheduled to be built just below the confluence of the streams. The cemetery will of course be moved to higher ground. Its site and that of the town will be the most deeply immersed of any to which this fate has been assigned. At low water it will be more than four hundred feet down.

Button Willow

In mournful windswept isolation this place is in a class all its own. It lays in a shallow bowl along a little watercourse on the eastern edge of that endless line of low rolling grass covered hills that lay between the Sierra foothills and the valleys of the Sacramento and the San Joaquin, called by former generations the Wild Goose Plains.

Several gold dredges were operational in the area in the not too distant past, solid evidence that a town could have supported itself in placer operations. No building or foundations are discernible or have been for years past. In anything documentary, we have just about nothing.

The late Al Wallen, who was fifty years afield as a geologist in search of alumina and non-ferrous minerals, informed me that an overly large proportion of his collection of artifacts, some of which are presently displayed in the San Joaquin County Museum, were retrieved at Buttonwillow and in close proximity thereto. These are almost entirely Mexican and Chinese in origin. Understandable when we recall that the owners of the Arroyo Seco, within whose boundaries it lies, were quite hardnosed toward the Anglos.

Near the head of the little watercourse, on its south slope, a small tunnel, long since caved in, trickles water down to the stream bed. This must have constituted the town water supply.

Shading it, a living thing, something that is entirely too plausible, apropos, and appropriate. In its symmetry and great size one may feel sure that it witnessed the birth of the community, its heyday, decline, and extinction, there is not another of its species within ten statute miles. A giant buttonwillow.

Poverty Bar

To Poverty Bar was granted ten short years of life. Within this brief span its enormous wealth nourished Lancha Plana and all of the complex of communities adjacent. The great flood of 1861-1862 visited upon it complete extinction. All bridges and ferries over the Mokelumne disappeared. In the thirty foot rise of the river, the roaring torrent, acting the part of a monitor, tore the stone buildings to pieces after it floated out the wooden ones. Old miners have told me that after that visitation of nature, practically all of the pay ground in the vicinity was just not there any more and such fragments that could be identified were, in some manner, seemingly leached of anything worth an effort of recovery.

This terrible winter was used by Bret Harte as a backdrop for the best tale ever to come from his pen: "How Santa Claus came to Simpson's Bar." He quotes the editor of the *Red Dog Clarion*, who observed with melancholy pride that: "an area greater than that of all of the New England States is now under water in the Valley of the Sacramento, San Joaquin."

When the waters finally receded there was hardly a recognizable feature of the landscape remaining.

Its site, until covered by the rising Lake of Camanche, was a flat bar of sand, many feet in depth, clean and sharp, in extensive use for miles around as a component of mortar and stucco. We must now turn to other sources.

What do we possess of Poverty Bar will be existent for a long time; at least parts of it will. This is the Poverty Bar Ditch, constructed by McNeely, Davis, Morrow, and McCarty. This was completed in 1857 and brought water over to the Amador side at a point near the Butler Claim by means of a suspension flume ninety feet high. Thus the two water systems, the Poverty Bar Ditch and the Lancaster Ditch were in direct competition, the result being a reduction in the price of water at the sluices. An absence or a shortage of water was the bane of all of the diggings. Thus the luxury of choosing between two rival sources was unusual if not unique. It is very highly improbable that this happened anywhere else, in either the northern or the southern Mines.

This ditch hugs the south wall of the Canyon of the Mokelumne for mile upon mile. A portion of it is now deep beneath the waters of Lake Pardee but the remainder is visible down the gorge to a point opposite the masonry headings of the old Morrow Bridge.

Ninety thousand dollars in those days must have had considerable purchasing power. This is a thing of beauty. Hundreds of feet of it are cut into greenstone harder than the hubs of hell. Great stretches of it are supported at the lower side by a stone wall in places more than fifty feet high.

We must not forget that the tools that produced this were pick and shovel, sledges, single jack drills, wheelbarrows, and black powder. How fortunate that no one bothered to tell the builders that their task was impossible until after the job was done.

Copper Center

The genesis of this place was identical with the Mc-Nealy mine at Muletown, Ranlett, and Townerville. The quest for copper and a strike of this metal in the lower reaches of Copper Gulch, under the terrific demands of the Civil War, brought into being stores, hotel, saloons, boarding houses, and the installation of extensive machinery for the exploitation of the vein.

A company named "The Star of The West" opened offices here and did a brisk business in the sale of the stock. Contemporary news items—or rather those of a few months—later remark rather ruefully that these stock sales were something that the company did real well: Production; not so good.

If we match the plaints of the singed investors with what is now known about the mineralogy of the place, it probably comes to this: One of the kidneys of very rich ore was discovered and exploited in the manner mentioned in the bit on Townerville. This triggered the speculation which fizzed out when the pocket was exhausted. Some contemporaries are bitter in their comment upon the would-be and prospective millionaires who hit camp in an expansive mood and, some weeks later, were hard put to scratch up subsistence and a ticket on the Butterfield Stage Lines to points east.

Probably no town died more quickly and more completely than this one.

Mason tells of the great windmill up on Bull Run Hill that was visible for miles around and a landmark for many a year. It must have been gone long years before the turn of the century for it was not remembered, even years ago, by anyone.

This site is at least a hundred feet deeper than that of Townerville beneath the surface of Lake Pardee.

For some evidence that it once existed, we are in better shape than we are with Union Bar and Columbia Bar. Copper Gulch, in the lower reaches of which the strike was made, is still on the maps of the U.S. Geological Survey, where it heads into the rugged contours above water line. So we will forever have the name of this gulch upon the map as the line of a sort of marker buoy to a place where dreams never came true.

Blood Gulch

In this piece of nomenclature Amador possessed a parallel or an equal, in the realm of the macabre, to Los Muertos in the south environs of Angels Camp in our adjoining county of Calaveras. At that site, eight men were found murdered along the bank of a stream which the Sonorian miners named most appropriately, el Rio de los Muertos.

Southwest of Fiddletown, in the same month in 1849, several victims of murder were discovered along a little stream to which the above chilling title was promptly fastened. The contrast here to the open-handed camaraderie, mutual trust, and helpfulness of the miners of the "Little Rush" of the summer and autumn of 1948, was shocking. Under the pressure of the common peril, vigilante units were formed throughout the mines to mete out justice and extend some measure of protection to the individual miner. In the heat of action it appears to be true that, in some cases, excesses were committed but that for the most part, a most unpleasant but quite necessary task was accomplished.

More than a century later armchair moralizers condemn these actions in the most scathing terms. One cannot help but wonder what their reactions would have been had they been present in a time and at a place where the Spanish and Mexican law had gone and the American law had not yet arrived: no courts, law enforcing agencies, places of detention, or any machinery existent whatever for the restraint of criminal conduct.

Spearheading the influx of undesirables were the ducks of Sidney Town and the escapees from the convict settlements of Australia.

In 1850 a group of miners at work at the sluices noticed a trail of blood in the water. Going immediately upstream around a bend they found the body of a miner slain short minutes before. This together with the events of the previous year riveted the grisly label to the watercourses quite permanently. In sequence now, one notes a fact that so often recurs in history and is entirely inexplicable. That a locale obtaining notoriety for some dark reason will perpetuate its bad name in the same manner as that in which it was acquired. The news media of the years immediately following list crime after crime committed in the gulch.

No scrap of evidence survives that any of the above was in the slightest degree a deterring factor in the building of cabins and shelters of various kinds at different points along the miles of the length of the gulch. Had any of the builders been susceptible to even a tiny bit of faintheartedness, they never would have made it to where they were.

The record of the time indicates that several nuclei of population shifted, regrouped, and drifted from month to month along the entire length of the stream.

Beyond a few house foundations it is most doubtful that any remains of a town are identifiable. Its disappearance is hardly exceeded by any of the others in its entirety and completeness.

Quien Sabe?

In a triangle blunted at the apex by Highway 49, bounded on the north by Dry Creek, and on the south by Sutter Creek, and based on the west by Highway 124, we have a sort of lost world in which remnants of old buildings and works of man, many of unknown purpose, are more numerous than in any other part of the county.

It is entirely cow country. Lone ranch establishments are few and far between. Dense thickets of chemise, live oak, valley oak, toyon, and digger pine together with ridges, hogbacks, ravines, and gulches cut the grazing areas into a crazy quilt of every size and shape. They also mask and conceal old shafts, stone walls, stone buildings, caved-in drifts and the myriad evidences of the great wave of humanity that, after its subsidence, turned all back to the forces of nature.

This is a dangerous area to enter in places, even for the owners of the ranches. A drift caved to just below the surface, or a shaft unknown to any now living; its opening masked by vegetation or a fallen tree, constitutes a mantrap of deadly effectiveness.

All evidence that can be assembled from sources documentary and legendary, place, in an area just south of Horse Creek and north of the present Preston reservoir, a population in the 1850's of between one and two thousand. At its nucleus all kinds of business establishments thrived and expanded.

Now here is our difficulty. It does not have a name. Digging in the libraries, afield, or in the reminiscences of old timers over many years, yields the same result. Who knows? It is clearly established that it was mostly Spanish speaking.

In an endeavor to establish a center we may examine a stone ruin situated about midway between the Goffinet and Tonzi roads.

Here, the walls of a building abandoned for more than a century are three feet thick, with a sort of maze of walls in the cellar or basement the purpose of which is not discernible. The stones in this opus are most of them a size that must have required a crane or shears to get them into place.

Impressive as this is, it is outclassed by a wall on three sides that was eight feet high and two-and-a-half feet thick inclosing, with the building at center rear, an area of at least an acre. When one raises a wall higher than five feet it passes from an animal barricade to a stopper of humans and of bullets. Some such goal must have been here to justify the greatly increased labor.

It is perhaps more helpful to understand these statements of wall height, thickness, and cubage if, as anyone who has ever turned a hand to the trade of masonry knows, even in building a garden wall, that we translate it into sore muscles, sprained ligaments, liniment, and back plasters. This way it comes out much more impressive.

We do not know who built this. We do not know for what purpose. We do not know how many tired backs it produced.

The name of the place, who knows? So let this be its name "Quien Sabe."

Journey's End

What did we miss? Infinitely more than will ever be set down on paper. What tales have these formless mounds of earth—that once shielded from the elements inhabitants whose physical entities are now a century returned to the good earth—to tell us that will never be told?

Since a number of people were in contact, all of the elements of tragedy, comedy, and drama that were raw material for the playwrights from Euripides through Juvenal, the Bard of Avon, Eugene O'Neill, and Arthur Miller were present and operational.

How many adult delinquents, low in funds and lower in character broke out the Walker Colt and went over to put the hoist on the town bank? How many employees scooped out the till and, when last seen, were going thataway? How many celebrants, homeward bound and thoroughly stoned, fell in through the wrong doorway? How many gentlemen at large escaped a fracture of the neck by being good judges of horseflesh and traveling lighter than the purusing posse comitatus. How many ladies departed camp in the small hours of the morning with individuals not their lawfully wedded spouses? How many claims, hardrock and placer, were salted? How much sympathy was extended to the purchasers of these claims?

We can never hope to know. But this we do know. The overwhelming majority were good people, men and women who endured as the rock Petrus, did their duty as they were given the light to see it, helped the unfortunate, established the rule of law against unspeakable odds and were doers of the Word.

They founded a great state and bequeathed to those of us who came afterward a heritage that we do so very little to perpetuate or defend.

Our Revels Now Are Ended

Our revels now are ended, These our actors,
As I foretold you, were all spirits, and
Are melted into air, into thin air;
And, like the baseless fabric of this vision,
The cloud-capped towers, the georgeous palaces,
The solemn temples, the great globe itself,
Yea all which it inherit, shall dissolve,
And, like this insubstantial pageant faded,
Leave not a rack behind. We are such stuff
As dreams are made on, and our little life
Is rounded with a sleep.

The Tempest   —William Shakespeare

Index

136